RESCUED BY THE ALIEN PIRATE

MATES OF THE KILGARI

CELIA KYLE

ATHENA STORM

THE ATHENAVERSE STAR CHART

BLURB

I woke from cryostasis a prisoner. My crime? I have no idea.

I was stuck with a hundred other women, all headed to who knows where. Captive in a dank, dirty cargo hold.

Then, out of the darkness, came Solair.

A handsome alien. Golden skinned. Horned. The dashing captain of a pirate ship. They rescued us--he gave my people food, shelter, and promised us safety. In exchange?

He took me for himself.

But the people who captured us, haven't given up. They want us back. They're powerful and will do whatever it takes to find us. The only thing stopping them?

Solair.

He wants me. And what he takes…

He keeps.

THE STORY SO FAR...

THE YEAR IS 2338. HUMANITY HAS WEATHERED IT'S infancy and has navigated to the stars. They've colonized other worlds and become a space faring civilization and formed the Interstellar Human Confederation.

Along the way, they've come to discover that the galaxy is actually a pretty crowded place. There are several political entities in the galaxy.

The Trident Alliance is composed of the Vakutan, the Pi'rell, and the Alzhon.

The Ataxian Coalition is composed of the Odex, Kreetu, Grolgath, and Shorcu.

The Coalition and the Alliance has been fighting a war for about 350 years. At its heart, it's an existential conflict that determines whether the known galaxy will be guided by the teachings of the Ataxian religion or by the capitalistic and technocratic tendencies of the Trident Alliance.

Details are unclear how the war between the Alliance and Coalition started, but atrocities in the name of protecting the innocent have been committed by both sides.

Several races, trying to remain neutral and unaffiliated with either side have formed a loose political union known as the League of Non-Aligned Races. Each race maintains their sovereignty. Member states meet infrequently to discuss trade and security matters, but no true leadership exists.

Many races over the centuries have settled and created a political entity known as the Helios Combine, situated between Coalition and Alliance space and next to the Badlands - a region of space with many stellar phenomena. The Combine is known for it's slave based economy, its capitalist based caste system, and a rigid social class system.

Humanity had for a long time maintained their neutrality, but after multiple encounters, sided with the Alliance in their war against the Coalition.

War has been unkind to the humans.

The IHC colony of Luvon, with over 2 billion people on it, fell to the ruthless race known as the Kraaj. The Kraaj had been loosely aligned with the League of Non Aligned

Nations but they saw the encroaching Coalition presence on their border as too dangerous.

They took the human colony to serve as a forward base of operations. In the process they brought much pain and misery upon the humans they had become the overlords of.

The Coalition has opened its offensive on Luvon now, and countless people are in the cross hairs.

The Alliance and Coalition have fought battles over the human planet of Armstrong. Once thriving, it is now a wasteland. A small group of survivors from both sides attempts to carve out a path of peace in the galaxy.

The war has been brutal. It has altered the trajectory of billions of sapient beings. One such race is what is known today as the Reapers. They're world, known as Oshara, was destroyed when they were forced to take sides in the Alliance-Coalition War. With their planet destroyed, they wandered for many years, looking for a home or refuge. Yet no power would allow them into their borders. Starving and at death's door, they pleaded to be allowed to settle and serve within the worlds of the Helios Combine. They were rebuffed by the arrogant and feudal Combine leadership. They eventually settled in a region of space known as the Badlands, surviving for generations as space pirates. With the war distracting attentions elsewhere, the Reapers are coming to realize that revenge against the Helios Combine is within reach.

Humans now navigate a galaxy that only offers fear, death, and destruction.

In a galaxy that's ripped apart by war, the only light is that one day, a measure of hope will be given to the hopeless.

That day has yet to come...

CHAPTER ONE

VARIA

The lights keep flickering on and off. I'm trying to hold it together and not let the darkness get to me, but I've never been comfortable in pitch black. Real darkness is like an abyss. If someone stares into it for too long, they'll go crazy, and I need all my wits about me to figure a way out of this mess.

"We've been stuck in this hold for seven days now," Lamira murmurs to me.

"If we even know what a day is," I reply, unable to suppress the bitterness in my voice or the twist to my lips. "They took my comms and timekeeping devices before shoving me into cryosleep."

Whoever "they" were, neither of us know.

For days now, I've been stuck in the hold of what appears to be a transport ship. I jerked awake to find myself in the dark, lying in an open cryopod. There's barely any food or water and no one around to explain what the hell I'm doing here. I'm starving, dehydrated, and pissed because I hate not knowing the full details of a situation, especially one that involves me.

And now the fucking lights keep flickering in and out.

"At least we're not alone," I sigh.

"No." Lamira grins. "We're surrounded by one hundred and seven women, nearly half of which are still in cryosleep and haven't woken yet. With very little food and water and one working toilet with no privacy."

She's right. We're stuck here and no one has any clue *why* we're here. Some woke after me, with questions I can't answer. I don't know whether to envy them or pity them because our situation is just that fucked up.

The last thing I remember before waking inside one of those pods is being arrested by Interstellar Human Confederation Security on planet Erebus while on my way to the store.

They didn't read me my rights. They didn't charge me with any crime.

I'm a human being, and a citizen of the Interstellar Human Confederation. I know no matter what I may have done I should have at least been told what crimes I was accused of.

They just grabbed me, threw me into a hovercar and hit me in the back of the head.

The next thing I remember is waking in a cryopod.

It took me a while to figure out my surroundings once I had the strength to get up. I'd stumbled around and found some food tucked in the corner, but it wasn't until I called out that other women woke.

That was several days ago.

All we've had a chance to do is... nothing.

We can't get out of this hold and that's left a lot of time to think.

I'm definitely not what one would call innocent, having dabbled in a bit of black-market trading, but I've never done anything serious enough to warrant detention and shipment off-world. That kind of treatment is usually reserved for the real assholes—murderers, marauders, and madmen.

Last time I checked, I'm none of those things, so how in the hell I ended up here is a mystery.

I don't even recall making it to interrogation. I was just

being grabbed by some IHC Security goons and then nothing. Blackness. The abyss.

Remember what I said about real darkness?

I'm trying hard to hold it together for the others. My resolve is unravelling quicker as time passes, but I'll be damned before I let anyone else know. As far as I can tell, those of us who are awake have been conscious for roughly seven days. But that's just a guess. The room is windowless and there are no tech devices for us to call up any type of calendar or ship's log. There's barely even any sound, save for the buzzing of the damn lights, random conversations, and occasional whimpers emanating from some of the women.

It's no surprise that they're starting to fall apart. While I'd been the first to waken, others soon followed, and then utter pandemonium ensued. Some of the women sobbed, some yelled, and worse, some did nothing at all, almost catatonic with shock. Using my most authoritative, take-no-bullshit voice I was able to calm everyone down long enough to discover I'm the only one aboard with any sort of military training. Because of that, I've become the de facto leader of our ragtag group.

Not that I mind. I'm good at giving orders. Sometimes I'm not the best at taking them, but I left the military honorably, so I don't feel too badly about that.

The good news is I've got a great team. Whoever locked us

up in here clearly didn't think through all the ways their plan could go sideways. My core group of girls each have a very specific skillset that will benefit us in the long run if we ever get out of here. I know I sure as shit wouldn't have put a former military sergeant, a tech geek, a mechanic, and a biologist together on the same transport.

Honestly, they're damn lucky this rig is locked up tighter than a space navy knot and we haven't yet figured a way out because once we do, there's no place in the galaxy they'll be able to hide where we won't find them. I'll make damn sure of that.

Water was more difficult to locate, but thanks to a resident genius and tech wizard from Novaria who introduced herself as Fiona, we have a small supply. Somehow, she rigged the pipeline to the stasis pods, allowing it to divert a small amount of water suitable for drinking. I have no idea how she did it because my brain doesn't work that way. It really doesn't matter how she accomplished the miracle—just that she did. She's proven herself to be a definite asset.

After we'd accumulated our stash of sustenance, I had Ilya, who'd informed me she was a professionally trained gearhead from Glimner, recon the entire hold. She'd spent hours crawling around on her hands and knees looking for a way out of this place. Despite all efforts, she'd come up short. Whoever put us here sure didn't want us leaving anytime soon.

The rest of my squad is composed of Thrase, who's lived on Mars and was a biologist. She's been monitoring the vitals of each of us, awake or asleep. There's Marion, a cook from Luvon who worked on Erebus before she too was taken and has shown she's quite capable of slapping together a meal of things you'd never think of mixing from the pile of food I located when I first woke. Then there's Lamira, originally from Titanus Vox, lately of Erabus with me and my best friend in the galaxy. She was with me when I'd been picked up and I'm afraid it's my fault she's here.

What I'm most confused about is how she ended up here with me. Even if I'd been arrested due to my transactions on the black market, Lamira is the cleanest whistle I know. There's no reason at all for her to be here.

She'd be so disappointed in me if she knew I'd been dealing. Keeping it a secret from her now will take some finesse. My primary concern is keeping her safe and getting her out of here alive because if she's in this mess due to me, I'll never forgive myself.

My breath stalls in my throat when the lights go out again. Silently, I count the seconds as they pass, dread filling my guts as they turn to minutes. We're in the dark for a full ten before they return in a blinding flash, accompanied by a series of echoing gasps and sighs of relief.

"Varia, a word?" Ilya keeps her voice low, not speaking until our heartbeats have returned to normal.

I nod and follow her away from the main group. Her lips are set in a grim line.

"Now clearly I'm not one hundred percent sure what's going on—" she starts, but I cut her off.

"Shoot straight, girl. If you know anything, you know we don't have time for bullshit," I tell her.

My voice is stiff but I'm smiling. In the days we've spent together my core group have quickly become close, knowing we've got to trust each other fully if we want to get out of here alive. I may be direct, but I genuinely care about these women and I think they know that.

Ilya returns my grin although hers is smaller and doesn't reach her eyes. "The lights going out intermittently signifies the issue with the ship is electrical in nature. Once they're out for good we'll lose whatever life support we have quickly," she gets the last out in a rush.

I stare into her baby blues, looking for fear but finding only rage.

"How long?" How long will we live once that happens?

"Group this size? Hours. A day at most."

Fuck.

"Thanks, Ilya. Keep this between us," I instruct, and she agrees with a nod. No sense in causing a massive panic.

I did not survive the firefight on Horus IV to go down like

this. I will not die like a rabbit in a trap, snared because I didn't keep up my guard. There's got to be a way out of here. We just have to find it.

Returning to the group, I ask Fiona to revisit the locking panels on all of the doors to see if she can bring them back to life. Just as she rises to do so, the lights go out again.

The amount of time we spend in utter darkness is longer this time. The cries of the women are louder, echoing throughout the high-ceilinged room. I wrap my arms around my chest and will myself not to fall apart. I keep my eyes closed as if to trick my brain into believing I'm not trapped inside a hulking metal coffin, quickly on its way to becoming a mass grave.

Watching everyone else start to give up is affecting me more than I thought it would. It's been days with no sign of anyone knowing we're here. The cavalry isn't coming. We're all going to die here. Mother save us, 'cause somebody has to.

When the lights come back on again this time, they're accompanied by the sound of a distant but resounding crash that shakes the entire ship. I reach out for Lamira, grabbing her hand in mine and pulling her close. Once the dust settles the silence returns, but only for a few minutes. The next sound we hear is closer—a rumbling, screeching noise that sets my teeth on edge, coming from outside the main doors.

"Fiona, *move!*" My scream reaches her just in time.

She darts out of the way as the doors burst inward, letting in a rush of fresh air. An unfamiliar deep male voice cuts the silence of the room.

"What the fuck is this?"

CHAPTER TWO

SOLAIR

"Uh, Solair? You might wanna come see this," Swipt calls out to me from his place in the pilot's seat aboard my ship, the *Ancestral Queen*. The tone of his voice tells me he's located something interesting, so I double-time it to him.

He and I, along with the rest of the crew of one hundred and fifty Kilgari males, are on our way back from a smuggling run to Glimner that couldn't have gone better. The cargo hold is lighter, our coffers are heavier, and I'm much happier than I was when I woke this morning.

Everything has been relatively quiet, so I wonder what's gotten Swipt's attention. He's hunched over his navigation panel, eyes narrowed as his fingers fly over the glass.

"What have you got?" I lean down to look over his shoulder.

"Distress beacon from an IHC freighter. The *Frontier*. The signal's weak, but it says they need immediate assistance," Swipt reports.

"What are the ship's specs?" I straighten and cross my arms over my chest.

"She's massive. Just shy of five hundred feet. Looks to have at least nine decks. Not sure what it's transporting. I've tried pulling it up on the flight database but there's only bare bones information. It's coming from Erebus but that's all I know."

"Are you sure it's IHC?"

Ninety nine point nine percent of IHC ships would be fully registered in the flight database, logging all pertinent information including what they carried. The fact that this one's not following protocol is either a red flag or a gift from the Precursors.

"That's what the computer says it is. No reason to believe it's wrong. Besides, it looks like it's one of the old Titian-class ships, so you know that's got to be IHC. They're the only ones who run those hunks any longer."

He's not wrong. The IHC rarely changes ship designs. It makes them all the more recognizable.

"What do you wanna do?" he looks to me.

I take a moment to think. I hold too many lives in my hands to make rash decisions. "Does that fancy computer of yours tell you how many are on board?"

Swipt scrolls through the report. When he finally speaks his voice is filled with disbelief. "It's reporting a crew of thirty."

Okay, now I know something's up.

"Thirty? On a vessel that large? Either your computer's borked or someone's lying. A partially registered IHC freighter with a skeleton crew all the way out here in League space? I'm not buying it. Set a course," I tell him. My decision is made and anticipation makes my blood sing in my veins.

"Yes!" Swipt exclaims and punches the coordinates into his command console. "I love when you're impulsive like this! Arrival in ten minutes."

I head to the comms station and pick up the intercom, advising my crew that we're taking a little detour. If my hunch is right, we're about to stumble upon a payload of salvageable cargo.

It doesn't get any better than this.

As we clip toward the *Frontier*, my first mate, Grantian, appears on the bridge beside me.

"What have we got?" he stares out of the massive viewscreen

before us at the stars racing by. He stands in his typical pose, arms crossed over his chest, mouth set in a grim line. Before he joined my crew, he was part of the Kell Hounds mercenary outfit and from the look of the scars that crisscross his body, he's not someone to be met on the dark side of any moon.

"A gift, I think," I tell him.

He snorts in response. "Hope you're right. Remember the last time you acted on a hunch? We almost didn't make it off Gur alive. Damn Coalition bastards..."

"Those Coalition bastards just paid your salary for the next month with our last run, so watch your tongue," I tell him. "Never forget that we're equal-opportunity pirates. We go where the gold is."

Grantian only nods, but I know *he* knows I'm right.

"Initiating coupling sequence. Gimme two minutes and we'll be locked," Swipt reports as the *thump* and *thud* of our connection to the *Frontier* begins.

"Go rally the troops, Grantian."

He gives me a mocking salute—we're not big on formalities in this outfit—and leaves the bridge to wrangle my core group of warriors. I trust no one in the galaxy more than Grantian, Swipt, Montier, Zandar, Lokyer, Nicari, and Kintar, and there's no way in fuck I'm heading onto a sketchy IHC freighter without them. Whenever

17

shit goes awry, it's always when they're not with me. I'm not risking it this time.

Once the *Queen* has successfully coupled onto the loading bay of the *Frontier,* I make the call to board. As soon as my foot touches down onto the other ship my suspicions are confirmed. Something's not right. It's eerily quiet inside, like a tomb. The engines have been shut down, so it's merely floating in the black of space.

"Montier, find out what's happened here. Check their logs," I tell him.

If anyone can figure out what's up with this place, it's Montier. He's a world-class engineer with a brain that never quits. If he doesn't know something, you can bet your horns no one else does either.

He pulls out a data pad and begins typing furiously, trying to hack into the ship's digital memory core. By the look on his face, it's not going well.

"Core's buggered. I can't get in. I don't have access to anything—comms, locks, controls, life support—nothing. But this is strange..." his voice trails off.

I know that tone.

"Focus, Monty, what's strange?"

"All the ship's energy is being diverted to the hold." He finally gives me his attention.

This situation just keeps getting more fucked with each passing second. There's absolutely no reason for all the ship's energy to be going to its hold—unless there's something alive down there. A big something.

"Do you at least have access to a map?"

"Negative," Montier's reply is immediate.

"Well then, let's haul ass," I tell them.

I gotta give credit where it's due. Even though it seems like this situation is about to go tits up, they follow me without hesitation.

Navigating the narrow hallways of an unfamiliar ship lit only by emergency lighting isn't easy. We get lost a few times, but with Montier's uncanny knack of finding his way around, we always end up headed in the right direction. I make a quick diversion to the bridge, wanting to see if there's any crew left to stumble upon, but I immediately wish I hadn't.

Because they're all fucking dead. Every last one of them are in various states of very, very dead. The creepy part is there's no sign of what killed them.

I really hope it's not whatever's down in the hold.

We continue making our way down there anyway, not only because of the energy diversion but also because that's where the cargo will be. We're smugglers, after all, so Priority Number One will always be getting the goods.

Unsurprisingly, the doors to the hold are locked tightly, too. Montier tries working his magic one more time to no avail, so I bring in Zander, our weapons tech, to assist Grantian with breaking and entering. I'm a little concerned with what we'll find on the other side but not enough to turn back now.

Within moments they've used a saw and one of Zander's bolt guns to blast a hole clear through to the other side. They both back off as the smoke clears, allowing me to enter first.

What started off as a great day is quickly spiraling down into one big clusterfuck. Staring back at me is a large gathering of human women, wide-eyed and in all states of emotion. Some look confused, some are crying, and one actually passes out.

"What the fuck is this?" I'm unable to stop the words from tumbling out of my mouth.

No one answers me, but there's movement at the back of the group. The crowd parts to reveal a very tall, very beautiful woman, with flaming red hair, gorgeous brown eyes, and a body I definitely wouldn't mind running my hands over. She begins interrogating me immediately.

"Who are you? Where did you come from? Why are we here? Are you the bastards responsible for locking us up?" she demands, nostrils flaring.

I haven't had much experience with humans, but if they're all as hot-headed as she is, I don't think I want to.

"I'm sorry. I believe what you meant to say was, 'Hello, Captain Solair, thank you for arriving just in time to save me and my friends. How can we ever repay your kindness?' That's me, by the way. I'm Captain Solair, but you can just call me Solair. We're not a very formal crew. And your name is?"

Her jaw hangs open, eyes wide, in a look of shock. "You...you rescued us?"

I nod. "Yes, apparently we did. Now would you care to tell me what you were doing in here?"

"Where are we?"

"I think I'm the one asking questions, Miss…"

"Who are you?"

This is getting tedious.

"Look, Miss. We need to know why you're on this damn ship." I may let my frustration with the situation show a little bit because the human woman bristles.

"Are you kidding me right now? You come busting in here like a bad action holovid with no answers and expect me to be grateful? We've been locked in here for days!"

"Be that as it may, this ship is disabled and its crew are all dead. If you wish to leave here, my ship and crew are your only option, Miss...?"

She's going to give me her name, even if I have to force it out of her. Despite her misplaced ire, she's piqued my interest. Not only is she gorgeous, but she has a very unique scent that feels like it's reaching out and drawing me in. Her scent reminds me of the hills of Kilgar, of the twin suns rising on a crisp dawn as a breeze dances across the plains. Of...

As soon as I notice it, the thought hits me light lightning.

This woman. This human woman.

Could this be my *jalshagar*?

My fated one?

The one in the galaxy I am to mate with?

It can't be.

But every fiber in my body is screaming that it is so.

The concept of *jalshagar* is an old one. It harkens back many millions of years, to teachings our religious leaders say was handed down by the Precursors themselves through our Elder Scrolls when they seeded life on Kilgar.

It's an old concept that's almost fallen into the annals of history, but one my father taught me when I was very young. In our common era most people choose their mate, but the Elder Scrolls of the Kilgar state that fated mates do exist, recognized at first by their scent, and confirmed upon the first shared kiss.

I can't imagine kissing this livid woman, but if she actually is my mate...

Yes, this day has definitely turned into a clusterfuck.

"Dawn. My name is Varia Dawn," she says a little sheepishly, as if realizing I'm not going to let up. "You can call me Varia. I apologize," she says the word through gritted teeth, as if it pains her to utter, "for coming at you like that, Solair, but you have no idea what we've been through. We're nearly out of food and water and... I'm a little on edge. I want to thank you nevertheless for rescuing us. I was so worried that these women were going to die on my watch."

"It's not a problem, Varia. Clearly we cannot leave you all here. You're more than welcome aboard my vessel, the *Ancestral Queen*. We have enough room to take you wherever you were going," I tell her. Though she will be going nowhere beyond my ship.

She furrows her brow, confusion on her features as she regards me. Her eyes look me up and down, lingering on my muscular chest and arms. Perhaps stupidly, I can't help but wonder if she likes what she sees.

"We have no idea where we were going." She shakes her head. "We... do you really not know anything about this ship?"

"We answered a distress call. You didn't activate the beacon?"

"Definitely not. As I said, we've been locked in this damn hold for days!" Her exasperation is growing again.

"Now, Varia, please be calm. I assure you, I'll help you sort this out, but I need you to work with me, not against me. Can you do that?"

I watch her as she eyes my crew interacting with the other women in her group. Our doctor, Nicari, has already begun initial assessments of the women, and she watches him the closest of all. Most of her comrades aren't as indignant as she is, seemingly grateful that we showed up when we did. They're chatting up the crew and even hugging them.

So many emotions cross Varia's beautiful face, but I can't get a read on any of them.

"Well?" I ask. I'm getting tired of waiting. I want to get the hell off this deathtrap ship immediately, even though my crew is about to get much, much bigger.

She eyes me like I'm a viper waiting to strike but finally nods her agreement. "Looks like the cavalry just arrived."

CHAPTER THREE

VARIA

While Solair's crew continues to bustle through the hole they cut into the hold, the Kilgari captain and I remain a few feet apart, staring at each other like angry cats.

Although let's be clear, he's a very, very dashing angry cat.

"I would just like to reassure you that my intentions are nothing but honorable." Solair's golden-skinned face stretches into a grin. "Besides, it seems to me that you don't have much choice but to accept our help."

He's right, of course, but that doesn't mean I have to like the situation. The galaxy is filled with regretful women who trusted the wrong sapient, and I'd rather not be one of them. After all the death and destruction that I've seen, I'm very wary of trusting anyone. One of the Kilgari, carrying a bulky case in one hand and a portable scanner pad in the other, pushes through his fellows and marches into the midst of my fellow survivors.

"Hey, stop that. What do you think you're doing?" I reach out and snag his sleeve as he runs the scan over the throng of *Frontier* women. His gaze snaps to me, and he licks his lips nervously before looking to Solair for support.

"You can relax, Varia. This is our ship medical officer, Nicari. He's just trying to help."

"Well, he needs to ask permission before he just starts scanning people at random. Hey, Ilya, what do you think you're doing?"

I gape as the mechanic, grease still staining her knees, elbows, and face, shakes hands with one of the tall, golden-skinned Kilgari crew. In my opinion, she's being much too friendly with a complete stranger. She turns her gaze on me, grinning from ear to ear.

"I'm just saying hello to Swipt here. Say hi to our captain, Swipt."

The handsome, lanky stranger smiles at me and offers a wave. "Hi to our captain."

I run a palm down my face, trying to contain my anger and frustration.

"First of all, I'm nobody's captain. Second, we all need to keep our distance until—oh for God's sake, Fiona, you too?"

The tech turns toward me and shrugs even as she stands near a Kilgari who has far more interest in her than I think is healthy.

"They're saving our lives, Varia. The least we can do is not be rude."

I look at my charges and find that Fiona and Ilya are not alone. All of the survivors who are out of cryosleep are now mingling with Solair's crew. In my mind, we were separated into two distinct lines—a carry-over from my days in the military—but I keep forgetting that the other women have no such experience. Despite the potential danger, they seem all too eager to embrace our would-be saviors.

The *Frontier* lurches hard to starboard, and only those of us with space legs manage to keep our footing. This means me, Fiona, the Kilgar crew and almost nobody else. I stumble a bit, but that cheerfully annoying Solair grabs my arm to steady me without asking.

"Easy." He cranes his neck, gold eyes scanning the walls as if he can peer through them to see the condition of the outer hull. "This ship is on the verge of coming apart. We need to get you safely aboard my ship, the *Ancestral Queen*."

"Hands off, buddy." I yank my arm out of his grasp, a bit miffed by how familiar the Kilgari captain is acting with me. What was with that weird look he gave me when we first met, anyway? I don't know a lot about the Kilgari race, so I don't have much frame of reference.

"I'm sorry, Varia. I only sought to help."

"So, you keep saying." The ship lurches again, and I rub the bridge of my nose and sigh. "All right, we have to get off of the *Frontier* while we still can. For the time being, we're going to accept your offer."

"Wonderful." He grins ear to ear, and for a moment I'm struck by the fact that if he weren't so overbearing and full of himself, he might be cute. Solair gestures grandly. "Please, if you'll come with us?"

I turn to the other survivors and raise my voice. "All right, listen up. We're evacuating this prison and taking Captain Solair up on his generous offer of refuge. Take anything that might be useful, but only what you can easily carry." I can't keep a grimace off my face as my gaze snaps back to Solair. "I swear to god, if this is some kind of trick and any harm comes to my people, I'll make you regret it."

"Your dedication to those under your command is highly commendable, Varia. Of course, you are right to be wary, but in this instance your suspicions are misplaced. The Kilgari are not Reapers, nor Gur slave traders. The Kilgari respect and admire women, perhaps more so than other sapient species because females of our kind are so very rare." His smile fades, and he quickly amends his statement. "That sounded like the ominous beginning of a bad holovid story. I assure you we are not looking to 'shore up' our supply of your sex—that is, of women—on our home world."

I bite back a nasty retort, trying to seem at least a little grateful, because like as not, they did just save our bacon. And to be honest, I want to trust Solair and his people—rough around the edges though they may be—but experience has taught me to withhold such trust until I have concrete evidence it won't be taken advantage of.

Our combined crew makes its way through the damaged, darkened corridors of the *Frontier*. When the freshly cut rectangle connecting our two ships appears, I remember the women still in cryostasis.

"Wait, Captain. What about the women who are still cryo'd?"

"Cryo'd?" He cocks his head to the side. "That didn't translate to Galactic Standard."

"You know, cryo'd—cryostasis." I shake my head, frustrated with what seems like my loss of control of this situation. "We can't just leave them behind."

Solair's eyes narrow with thought before he turns to one of his men.

"Montier, send an engineering team to facilitate the safe transport of the cryopods. Make sure they're in full environmental suits, or even class four hard armor, in case of a hull breach."

"Aye, Captain."

Solair returns his golden-eyed gaze to me and arches his brows high on his face. "I hope that will assuage your concerns, Varia."

"Yes, thank you."

We step through the cut-out section of the *Frontier's* hull and into the Kilgari ship for the first time. She's an older model, definitely built before I was born, but she seems sturdy enough. Here the odd cinnamon-esque tang of Kilgari body odor is stronger, but not overpowering.

I remain in the cargo hold as long as it takes to ferry the survivors aboard. It rankles me to see my fellow survivors mingling so freely and easily with the Kilgari crew while the cryopods are carried on, but there's not much I can do about it. I'm not even officially in command. It's just that no one else was stepping up to do it.

Marion, our de facto cook, elbows her way through the crowded throng to my side, her face crossed with worry. "That's all one hundred and seven of us, Varia, including those still in stasis, but I'm a little bit worried about them getting everything they need on a ship full of—ahem —men."

"Tell me what's on your mind, Marion."

I've come to rely upon Marion a great deal in our short association. While I might be the default leader of the survivors, Marion is our matron saint. Even with the limited supplies available in our prison, she's managed to keep us reasonably healthy and can work wonders with freeze-dried rations. Makes me wonder what she could do with actual ingredients.

"Of course, we need the essentials, like fresh clothing and basic hygienics, but ah… some of the women are on their cycle, so we need the products to deal with that."

Solair has been listening this whole time, and he motions for one of his men.

"Kintar."

A burly Kilgari, with arms as thick as docking chains, lumbers over toward us, his jaw set hard. He has a scar going over one eye, and I can tell from the way he carries himself that he's seen heavy combat. Our eyes meet and we exchange nods, a subtle recognition of one warrior to another.

"Kintar is our steward, tasked with providing basic sundries among other, varied duties. He will be more than happy to assist your woman Marion in her endeavor."

Kintar turns his jaded gaze on Marion and his eyes widen.

I could be mistaken, but his nostrils flare and the hard light in his eyes seems to soften.

"Marion, was it?" He offers his hand in the human salutatory greeting and Marion accepts, albeit with a cocked eyebrow.

"Ah, yeah, Marion it was. I mean, is."

"I am Kintar. Pleased to meet you."

I turn my troubled gaze upon the rest of my "crew" as Kintar leads Marion off into the bowels of the ship. They seem all too willing to blindly accept the Kilgari as our saviors, a fact which stings more than a little. But the final straw is when I see Lamira shyly gazing at a Kilgari officer when he's not looking. Likewise, when he thinks she doesn't notice, he gives her a longing, lingering stare.

I turn to Solair and cross my arms over my chest. If I return to IHC space, there's a good chance I'll be arrested again. I know I'm guilty, but Lamira is as innocent a soul as you're likely to meet. I need to get her name cleared and her life back, if at all possible—her and the rest of the women I've been looking after.

Who will look after them? I can't just let them fall to the whims of fate if I go with the flow. Not after everything I've been through.

This will not be like Horus IV again.

I know what I have to do. I need to take them home.

"Solair, I'm grateful for the rescue, but I'm afraid we can't remain on your vessel. None of us are even supposed to be here in the first place. We need shuttles to return us to our part of the galaxy."

CHAPTER FOUR

SOLAIR

My nostrils flare as I spin back to face this human woman. Once again, the unmistakable scent of my mate floods me and my brain reels. Surely not. This stubborn creature can't be the one. Can she?

"Say that again?" I've hardened my face into the most forbidding mask I can manage, willing her to surrender her argument on the spot. This look has conquered some truly formidable adversaries, but Varia? Her lips tighten further, and she clasps her arms firmly across her decidedly ample bosom.

"I said, we aren't supposed to be here. Now, I'd appreciate it if you'd have your men organize some shuttles to take us home. Or contact someone who can help us to do that."

A spark sizzles in my gut and that constructed grimace of control grits down into actual anger. There will be no pulling punches with this one. She gives as good as she gets.

My chest tightens as my teeth grind together so hard, I feel like they might crack. She stands as certain as anyone I've ever seen. Damnit. She's a match all right. I rock back onto my heels a moment before leaning in to give her the best I can manage.

"Does this look like a cruise ship?" It dawns on me that she hasn't seen more than a few square feet of the *Queen*, but I dig in my heels. "Take a look around. She's done true service, and has plenty more ahead of her, but it takes all hands to keep her running. Even in your state, you'll have to admit we're nowhere near equipped to just ship a hundred stragglers off on their merry way."

"One hundred seven," Nicari says while shepherding more of our new charges across the hold.

"Thanks, Doc. One hundred seven. Even you have to admit that it's a tall order to just tuck you into some handy shuttles, stock them with food, water, and fuel and wave you on your way."

"Well, you have to do something." There's an imperiousness, a certainty in the way that she speaks that cracks fire up my spine. Like I could throttle her and kiss her at the same time. I'll need to keep a handle on myself around this one. "I can't let my people down. No one knows why they were locked up in the first place! I need to help them!"

"Woman, 'have to' isn't something you get to say to me. And I'll thank you to remember you're speaking to the captain of this vessel."

"Pulling rank is a weak move, Captain."

Every drop of blood in my body turns to liquid fire. Forget the kissing part. It's taking every iota of will I can muster not to strike this dazzling creature down where she stands. I lean in close to her, quaking under my skin.

"Call me weak again."

Her eyes flutter, and a bit of steel melts out of her spine. It's a tiny concession on her part, but it's clear she's about to cede ground. And not a moment too soon, for my taste.

"I wouldn't." She shakes her head. "That was too far."

"That almost sounds like an apology."

"Almost." Her lips twitch.

She may have given an inch, but it's only an inch. I shake my head in frustration and suddenly become aware that we are the sole focus of a startlingly large circle of silent faces. Some are from my own crew, but the greater number are the thin, haggard faces of the women who have spent what must have felt like an eternity wondering how much longer they had to live.

Whether Varia has stopped to take them in or not, I can't say. It doesn't really matter. What does matter is that I have to reevaluate this steadfast woman opposing me. She just wants what's best for her own.

Less than ten minutes ago, they were looking to her as their leader, and now she's fighting to get them the best possible quarter. I've stood in those boots before. More than once.

Silence has settled in, and I can feel that every pair of eyes is resting on me. She's given about as much room as she's going to, and the ultimate decision lies in my hands. Pulling in a deep breath, I'm flooded yet again with the confounding odor of the mating bond. Great.

"Look. The *Ancestral Queen* just doubled her charge by bringing you on board. We can make it work, but it's going to take concessions on both sides. We're going to have to work together. If your women—"

"No concessions." She cut me off. I can't believe it. "Getting these women home is the first priority for me. I can't fail them. Please, I beg of you to help me."

"First, second, or last, it doesn't matter. We don't have the means. So, get comfortable."

Varia's mouth drops open at this.

I take advantage of her shocked silence. "We'll do what we can to get you where you want to go, but we're going to have to do it together. There aren't any shuttles to spare, much less provisions to send off with you. The situation isn't dire, but we're going to have to come up with a plan."

"I have over a hundred women who've been snatched from their lives with no memory. Do you know what kind of a violation that is? They had families and homes that they were just grabbed from. We all woke up with no memory of how we got on that ship and in that cargo hold. We need to get them back home. I'm grateful for rescuing us, but I'm begging you to help us get home."

"I'm sorry."

"That's not good enough."

"Good or not, it's what you're going to get. When I say no, no is what you're going to have to take. All the folded arms you can manage aren't going to make the impossible a reality." At my mention, she slackens her grip a bit and I can sense something like a truce creeping upon us. "That said, I'm open to suggestions. It's going to take some strategy to ensure we can stretch the food and water on board to keep everyone from getting at each other's throats."

"Even more at each other's throats," Nicari says from behind me. I'm tempted to wheel on him, but I've got bigger quarry at the moment.

"Fiona?" Varia calls out.

"Yes?" A lean woman behind me steps forward and Varia gestures to her.

"Maybe she can help. She's done as much as anyone to keep us all alive for the last few days. I'd say she knows her way around the technical side of things."

"That's a start." I'm keeping my eyes on Varia. If she wants to have some say, I'm going to make her earn it. "What else do you have?"

"Well, Marion has been stretching our rations."

"You're damn right, I have been." I turn to find a cranky-looking bundle of a woman already embroiled with Kintar and I recognize the look on the male's face. It mirrors my own. Preserve us all, this ship is about to be awash with mates.

"What we ought to do is lug the rest of that stuff onto this tub—whatever it's called. It may not be the most versatile stuff in the universe, but it'll be a damn sight better than nothing when the rest of the rations come up short."

My steward has been failing to settle her for the entirety of her short tirade. Kintar has seen some true service in his time, but I imagine he's going to have his hands full when it comes to this feisty human woman. Well, so be it.

"All right," I turn back to Varia, "you've identified two among your number who can make themselves useful.

The rest of you are going to have to prove yourselves." Again, just a bit more steel ebbs out of her resolve.

"Kintar, why don't you sort this crap out? I've spent more time than I can afford tangling with this... inconvenience." I make certain my gorgeous adversary knows I'm referring to her as I say this. "It's your problem now."

"Aye."

With a trim salute, I turn on my heels and listen to Mariah, or whoever she is, hectoring him about how best to do his job. She sounds so much like him I don't have the slightest doubt that his own nose is tingling with the scent of his true mate. Part of me wants to pity the poor bastard.

I would, if I didn't have a sinking feeling in my stomach with each step I take. My own siren song is wafting to me —growing fainter and fainter as I stride way. In the entirety of my spacefaring career, I've never retreated from anything. And yet, here I am, doing my level best not to break into a run.

Even when her smell is clear of my senses, I can't escape the imprint of her image in my mind. Her determination, her stubbornness, and her beauty all point to one clear conclusion.

This is going to be one serious battle.

CHAPTER FIVE

VARIA

After the exchange I'd had with Solair, I felt the need to put some distance between myself and the Kilgari captain. Which is just as well, since other people with other concerns are taking all of his attention at the moment.

I wind up stalking through the curving, burnished corridors of the *Ancestral Queen,* trying to create a mental map of its many decks just in case we have to try and escape. Not that the Kilgari have been anything but accommodating, of course, but I'm not ready to lower my guard yet.

One thing strikes me more than anything else. Solair wasn't kidding when he said that every single hand was needed to keep this relic flying. Everywhere I travel, there's always someone busy with one task or another. Usually they ignore me, but sometimes the Kilgari will glance up and stare, though when I make eye contact, they quickly look away.

As I walk around a crewman mopping up an apparent leak from a cooling line, my belly gurgles loudly. We'd been rationing our meager stores while trapped on the *Frontier*, so to be honest I'm more than a little peaked. For a time, I wrestle with my pride, telling myself there are more important matters than filling my belly, but when I start feeling lightheaded it becomes a matter of practicality as much as comfort.

Now, where did I see the kitchen, or mess hall, or whatever the Kilgari call it? Up on deck three, I believe. Guess the captain doesn't want to walk too far from his cabin to get a bite to eat—assuming that Solair keeps his quarters on the first deck as is standard protocol on most vessels. Not that I'm speculating about visiting his quarters, of course.

I get lost a couple of times, but eventually my nose brings me to the Kilgari mess hall. Following the scent of what I hope is a familiar Rauth stew, I traverse the twisting corridors. I start to pick up on the murmurs of conversation, which grow louder as I inch closer to my goal.

At last, I round a bend and come upon a pair of wide-open sliding doors, revealing a scene within of dozens of

Kilgari and many of my fellow survivors seated in clusters around the room. The women are shoveling the Kilgari fare down their gullets with abandon, which troubles me quite a bit. I hope they made the Kilgari taste it first in case it was poisoned.

I enter the mess hall, and despite the gnawing ache in my belly I don't head for the chow line. Instead, I visit the nearest table of survivors and crouch down next to them.

"Hey, how is everyone doing?"

"We're good, Varia. Better than good." A twenty-something wannabe musician named Lara digs her spoon into the gray-brown sludge of Rauth stew. "The Kilgari chef is amazing."

"Just remember not to gorge yourselves. Our stomachs have all shrunk due to rationing, and you have to stretch them back out slowly."

They nod their assent but continue to shovel food into their mouths with abandon. When we were trapped on the *Frontier*, the other women obeyed my directives almost without question. Now, it seems like I've been replaced, and it irks me though I know it shouldn't. I should be happy that my people are warm, fed, and have plenty of fresh air to breathe.

But I can't shake the feeling that I'm just not needed as much any longer. Maybe that's what drives me to visit each and every table full of survivors in turn to make sure with my own eyes and ears that they're doing well, and more importantly, being treated well.

While moving among the different clusters of my fellow survivors, I catch snippets of conversation all around the mess hall. The Kilgari are wary, keeping their distance for the most part. A few make comments about how nice it is to have women on board, though they don't seem to be of the creepy variety. More like a genuine appreciation. Perhaps with so few members of the opposite sex in their society we have become a kind of comfort, or novelty at least.

When I finally arrive at the last table of my fellow survivors, I grimace in frustration as I notice some of my people still missing.

"Has anyone seen Ilya? Or Fiona?" I don't see Marion, but I assume she's still busy trying to secure supplies for us from the Kilgari quartermaster, Kintar.

"Oh, they're hanging around with their new best friends, Montier and Swipt." One of the women giggles and then the entire table starts laughing. I spot Lamira near the head of the table and move over to sit next to her.

"Did I miss something? I don't get why this is funny." They should not be following the Kilgari crew around like puppies, especially when we don't know if we can trust them yet.

"Oh." Lamira's cheeks redden, and she glances over at the rest of the women and chuckles. "Ah…"

Lamira leans over and whispers in my ear. My mouth flies open and I stare at her in wide-eyed disbelief.

"What? They have *two*?" The table erupts in laughter at my expense, and heat rushes to my cheeks. "Not that it matters in the least, of course. This is a rescue operation, not a dating service."

As if on cue, Swipt comes sweeping into the mess hall, engaged in an animated conversation with Ilya. Both of them have dirt and grease on their clothing and somewhere Ilya has picked up a Kilgari tool kit, which she wears on a strap over her shoulder. She notices my glare from across the room but mistakes the reason for it. She waves and comes over, Swipt in tow.

"Varia, I've got great news. Swipt and I figured out how to boost the oxygen production in the life support systems."

"To be fair, it was mostly her idea." Swipt beams a smile at the lithe engineer, and I feel rather uncomfortable at what I see in his eyes when he stares down at her. "By increasing the temperature in our algae vat by just two degrees, she discovered that our oxygen production will increase by over twelve percent—perhaps as high as fifteen percent."

"It doesn't solve the problem, but it will help alleviate the strain on the systems." Ilya's smile fades when she notices my scowl. "Ah, is something the matter?"

I don't answer. I just shake my head and move on to the mess line. What's wrong with everyone? Why are they just so eager to trust a ship full of men who have no material gains to make by helping us? This is a privateer ship, meaning that it's all about making creds. Our sudden arrival can't have done anything but hurt their potential profits, even if it's just by taking up cargo space.

And yet, the Kilgari seem happy that we're here. Some of them joke about how much trouble we're causing and that everyone will have to put the toilet seat back down now habitually, but for the most part it's all good natured and not resentful.

I know I need to be vigilant. I know I may the only thing between their freedom and ending up on an auction block on a League world.

I will not let my people down again.

"Hey there. I'm told your name is Varia."

I turn my gaze away from the mess hall proper and focus it on the Kilgari standing at the head of the food line. He has an easy smile and a good amount of muscle popping out from behind his thin white apron.

"Varia it is. And you must be the mess officer."

He offers a slight bow, parting his hands out to the sides.

"Jax is my name. You must be famished. Command can really take it out of you. That's why I'm the happiest guy on the *Queen*. Nobody messes with the chef."

"It's the same on ancient Terran privateer vessels. Food is the one pleasure of a sailor, so it doesn't make any sense to turn the chef into your enemy."

Jax laughs as easily as he smiles. He spoons a ladle full of Rauth stew into a metal bowl and slides it across the counter to me. The aroma makes my mouth water and my belly gurgle louder than ever before.

"Sounds like you need to eat." He slaps a long, knotted pastry of some sort next to the bowl. "Here, this is *gatchi*, a hearty butter roll that I've personally tweaked to be chock full of dietary fiber and essential nutrients."

"Really? That sounds great." I bite off a piece of the end and chew, my smile slowly turning into a frown.

"I'm still working on the taste. But it is nutritious."

I try to smile and then thank him kindly before walking to Lamira's table and dumping the *gatchi* into the trash bin on the way.

CHAPTER SIX

Solair

I hope this whole thing doesn't turn out to be a disaster. Judging from what the security system shows, there's a great danger that it may. Screen after screen shows my crew squabbling, flirting, and generally being distracted by the human women infesting the ship.

Thanks to this new diversion, the bridge is deserted. Not that I mind. My brain is twisting around itself at such a rate that I'm grateful for the solitude.

On one feed, I can see Montier working away on the transport vessel. He's been charged with stripping it down for any supplies or equipment the *Queen* might be able to use. As efficient as he is, I imagine he'd be making better progress if a woman wasn't getting in his way at every turn. I click the audio for that sector to listen in.

"...just going to take everything?"

Montier sighs. "That's the order. Strip it to the shell." He tries to step around her, but she follows him.

"Disabling a vessel like this would be a crime."

"Who said anything about disabling?"

"Well, the rate you're going, she'll be completely destroyed within the hour." Montier drops his head a moment and then places his hands on his hips.

"So, what would you suggest? I'm under orders to recover anything essential for our own ship."

At the invitation, this woman plucks a wrench from Montier's belt and sets off, leading him along like some bashful recruit.

"Isn't that something?" Swipt has materialized over my shoulder and I start at the sound of his voice, embarrassed at being caught spying. "Have you ever seen Montier so out of his element?"

I shake my head, stifling my own feeling of kinship with the poor bastard.

"Which one is that," I ask. "What's her name?"

"Ilya, I think. She seems to know her way around a wrench."

He's not wrong. With a few deft strokes, she's managed to loosen a circuitry panel. She and my own engineer are hefting it toward the growing mound of plunder. Even with the blurry security images, I can tell the way they are looking at each other. A dull ache creeps up in my chest— could it be jealousy?

"What next?" Montier looks to her, and she takes a sweeping survey of the chamber before heading off in a decisive stride with the Kilgar trailing after. Swipt lets out a bleat of laughter.

"She's hilarious. Leading him around by his cocks. The man is a lost cause."

"What about you?" I've turned to face Swipt directly and the male's grin fades a bit at my query. "It seems like every member of my crew has caught the scent. Have you?"

"Maybe." There's something pensive in his expression that I recognize immediately. Maybe because I'm feeling it so acutely myself. "It's hard to say. Hopefully I'm not in as much trouble as that."

He nods back to the array and I follow his gaze to the dining hall feed. Clusters of my men are huddled around tables and you can bet there's a woman at the center of every orbit. I have to hand it to them; everyone looks like they're having a grand time.

Almost everyone.

In one corner of the screen, I can see Kintar locked in a decidedly animated exchange with several women, one of which I recognize is named Marion. With a couple of keystrokes, I silence the previous audio and engage the new one.

"If you think you can just divvy these women up among yourselves like the spoils of war, you might as well just load us right back onto the *Frontier*."

"I wouldn't mind being divvied up!"

"Shut up, Lara, I'm being serious."

"So am I!"

"Would you please listen to me?" Kintar's voice is teetering on the edge of genuine danger, and I can smell him trying to keep his temper all the way up here on the bridge. "It's like you're deliberately misunderstanding me."

"Is that so? You just said you wanted to quarter these women in the men's rooms."

"Again, I wouldn't mind," Lara breaks in.

"If you don't stop with that right now…"

"Everyone pipe down, *now*!" Kintar finally breaks, his voice so loud it makes the speakers crackle on our end. I've heard him bawl out like that before, so I can attest as to how impressive it is. In any event, he gets his wish.

Marion looks stunned and affronted in equal measure. Regardless, she keeps silent and lets Kintar have the floor.

"If you would let me finish before squawking over me, I'm trying to suggest that we double bunk some of you in the men's quarters and ask for volunteers among the crew to double bunk themselves. I've no doubt we'll find willing parties on both sides."

"It wouldn't accommodate everyone. There are over a hundred of us."

"Yeah, well, nearly half of you are still in cryostasis, so I think we can manage. For those who don't get rooms, we can make arrangements to clear out some unused cargo holds in the far end of the ship and try to make them comfortable."

"How are we supposed to decide who lands where? None of us can pull rank."

"I'm sure you'll think of something."

Swipt reaches past me and kills the audio and we sit in silence for a beat, watching the screens and the hive of men sent roiling by the new arrivals.

"Are you willing to double bunk, Swipt?"

"Perfectly willing," he says, "but I'd rather it wasn't with another member of the crew." It's the first hearty laugh I've had in a while, and I'm grateful for it. I know exactly how he feels. And I have no doubt he feels the same knotted gut I do, regardless of the quip.

"Captain, I'm heading down to see if Montier can use an extra set of hands. Is there anything specific you want me to do?"

"No," I wave him off. "Just don't get into too much trouble."

"What do you think my chances are?" And he's gone, leaving me to return to the thinly contained mayhem tickling across my security screens. This could be a huge disaster.

It was all well and good to play the hero, sweeping in to rescue these people, but I hadn't counted on the reality of a hundred women scampering around my ship. They're playing hell with the focus of my crew and breaking the authority of my command. I've never argued with anyone on board the way I did with Varia.

As if by instinct, my eyes find her on the screen. I barely have to look. I already recognize the rhythm of her gait.

She's in the dining hall, doing her best to wrangle her charges into some kind of order. Her firm stance and four-square directness acquire something akin to grace. She's a born leader. It's almost admirable at this distance.

Impossible as she is, I have to admit that she's a force to be reckoned with. We didn't exactly get started on the best terms, and I'm not exactly looking forward to our next conversation. It'll be tricky to explain to her that she might be my mate.

How do I even broach that kind of conversation with a human woman? I don't know the first thing about mating or partnering rituals among her people. Are they always as combative as all the apparent matches seem to appear?

I've heard a lot about humans. They are a relatively young race to the galaxy and have not been traversing the stars as long as the Kilgari or other races. But their remarkably short life spans mean they are constantly moving and changing things. They are never content to let the galaxy take them on their course. They must always be asking questions and discovering new things.

In the short time they've been in space, they've carved out impressive gains. In just a few short centuries, they've grown and expanded so that now there are roughly 140 billion human beings living on the worlds of the Interstellar Human Confederation. They've emerged as a power in this quadrant of the galaxy, and it's good that they have. They have very strong neighbors—with the Trident Alliance and Ataxian Coalition on their borders.

Perhaps not. On the screen, I can see Varia engaged in easy conversation with Jax. Something inside my stomach goes ice cold at the sight of them.

Many in our society do not believe in the Precursor myth

that has its stories in our Elder Scrolls. Either they are too modern, or they are unwilling to believe that an outside hand guided life on my planet. But the Scrolls have said since even before the Kilgari took to space one's mate need not even be Kilgari.

Before even we knew of other life on other planets, we've been taught that finding the one true mate was not relegated to our race.

Do humans engage in nonexclusive relationships? Even if we proved to be the ideal match, would I be expected to share her with other males as if she were a Kilgari female with multiple mates? In the past I've engaged with females in that easy manner, but this feels decidedly different.

"No."

I'm surprised at the sound of my own voice. Watching her slip out of her interaction with our mess officer, all I can feel is relief that their chat has drawn to a close. With each step she takes away from him, I breathe a little easier.

If I needed an answer, that was it. Not only am I completely taken with her, but I would do just about anything to ensure that she belonged to me alone. The whole question is moot until we share our first kiss. Only that will confirm whether we truly are the match that I'm afraid we might be.

Still. Given that all we've done up until now is spar for power, that first kiss seems like a long way off.

I let my focus return to the greater sweep of the security array. If there are true matches to be had, any number of my crew are well on their way to that first kiss. Several are already a damn sight closer than I am.

And, even if they aren't all matched mates, this ship is about to get a whole lot busier than it was a scant few hours ago. I only hope Varia doesn't get swept up into it as well.

CHAPTER SEVEN

VARIA

While I couldn't palate the *gatchi* roll, Jax's take on Rauth stew goes down easily—too easily. Despite my warning to the other women to take it slowly so as not to tax their shrunken stomachs, I wind up hurting myself on three bowls of the stuff.

Now that my hunger is sated—and then some—I check on the other survivors once more. A few of them have been toughing it out, but now that the constant threat of doom is no longer over their heads, the tears flow.

I try to bolster the morale of those who are in despair and thank those who are holding it together for everyone else. We're not exactly a homogenous group, coming from all different walks of life, but a sense of camaraderie permeates our every interaction. Maybe I'm afraid of that being diminished now that we're on the Kilgari vessel, and that's why it bothers me so to see the two groups beginning to intermingle.

Lamira comes to my side and puts her hand on my shoulder. When I turn to face her, her face is creased with a worried frown. "Take it easy, Varia. Sit down for a moment."

"I'm fine," I say that, but I also wipe sweat from my brow and my breath seems to be coming in rapid gasps. "Or maybe I'm not. We must have been in cryosleep long enough to suffer the beginning of muscle atrophy, or at least I was. I wonder if the Kilgari have a gymnasium or some such?"

"You could ask Solair." Lamira's eyes glitter with hidden meaning. "He seems... helpful."

"Get that stupid grin off of your face." I slap her hand in mock anger, mostly to cover up the fact that my cheeks feel warm all of a sudden. Yes, Solair is a devastatingly handsome sapient—I am even getting used to his horns— but that doesn't mean I trust him as far as I can throw him.

"All I'm saying is, sometimes the Galaxy throws you an opportunity." She shrugs, her oh-so-innocent eyes dancing with not-so-innocent thoughts and innuendo.

"I'll show my foot an opportunity in your keister..."

My words die out when I see Marion enter the mess hall, the quartermaster Kintar not far behind. Funny, I just noticed that Kintar's horns aren't very small, as I initially believed, but filed down. I wonder if that's significant or just a personal taste?

In any event, Marion scans the room until she locks gazes with me. Then she sidesteps and shoulders her way through the crowded room to my side. I can tell from the lightness in her stride and the way her eyes are lit up that she has good news.

"Varia, Kintar and I have managed to secure sleeping quarters for all of the survivors."

A smile stretches across my lips, and I put a hand on her shoulder. "That's good news, Marion. Thank you so much for facilitating this."

"Kintar did most of the work. I just stood around being demanding." She chuckles and then her face creases with worry. "There's a few caveats, of course."

"I expected as much. It's not like this is a luxury liner bound for Glimner."

"She's a good ship, Varia. Of that I have no doubt, as I've been on quite a few." Marion gestures at the throng of women at the mess hall tables and sighs. "One of the caveats we were kind of expecting. We'll have to double and even triple up on rooms."

59

I shrug because at the moment having a roommate seems a small price to pay to avoid suffocation and starvation.

"After being cooped up together in that tiny hold on the *Frontier*, it's going to seem like being on vacation. What else have you got?"

Marion purses her lips and I can see her making mental calculations. "Well, the holds aren't meant to quarter sapients, so they're on the cold and spartan side."

"We can solve that with extra blankets."

"Quite. But the main problem is that the Kilgari don't have enough bedding to go around. Kintar's come up with some cushions, so I guess we'll just have to make do."

I stroke my chin thoughtfully, trying to puzzle this latest conundrum out. While I'm sure we could make do, it would be far more comfortable to find an alternative.

Then it hits me. There should be plenty of bedding available—on the *Frontier*.

"Marion, do you know if the *Frontier* is still docked with this ship? Is she still holding together?"

Marion nods, and gestures toward the aft deck where the two ships are connected.

"Yes to both. Ilya and their engineering guy headed over to the *Frontier* to strip it for useful parts, and I think they figured out a way to stabilize it temporarily. Why do you ask? You're not considering heading back over there. Are you?"

The fear in her tone is plain. I suppose my gruffness and refusal to take the Kilgari at their word has led to some worry that I'd rather lead us back to a dying ship than remain here on the *Ancestral Queen*.

"No, I'm not. That ship would need a dry dock and about three months of intense labor just to be truly space worthy. But the bedding on board, on the other hand, should be just fine."

Marion's eyes light up, and her mouth drops open. She points a finger at me and grins.

"That's a great idea, boss. I should have thought of that. Do you think Solair will lend us a few hands to help transfer them over?"

I consider the idea of speaking to the Kilgari captain again, but I'm just not ready for that yet. Instead, I turn around and interpose myself between a Kilgari and the mess hall portal. He grinds to a halt, his eyes widening in query.

"Pardon me, but I need some help. Can you find about a dozen able-bodied Kilgari with nothing to do at the moment?"

His mouth opens silently, but he nods. The Kilgari moves over to a cluster of his fellows, casting one last glance my way before speaking with them quietly. In short order he returns, a bunch of muscled he men in his wake. Wow, they're being quite accommodating. I had expected more resistance.

"Excellent. We're going over to the *Frontier* and bringing back bedding for my people. Can you and your team manage that?"

"We will make you proud, my lady." The Kilgari bows his head respectfully and then heads out the door. I grab Marion's arm and point at the retreating Kilgari.

"Marion, go with them so you can show them where to take the bedding."

"Copy that, boss." Marion moves quickly after the Kilgari, her shorter stride not stopping her from catching up to them.

I'm considering heading over to the *Frontier* to help coordinate the transfer when I hear my name across the din of the mess hall.

Turning around, I find Solair walking toward me on stiff legs. His expression is akin to someone who has just bit into a fresh apple and found it's full of wriggling worms. Expecting a confrontation, I cross my arms defiantly over my chest and match his glare spark for spark.

"Is there something I can help you with, Solair?"

"Help me?" He blinks several times, eyes flashing with

anger. "I thought I was trying to help you, but it seems that you must test my patience, time and time again."

"What is it now? Look, if we're eating too much food—"

"I'm not concerned about your appetites, Varia. What troubles me is your propensity for ordering my men about—*my* men—as if they were your own."

I arch an eyebrow at him and shake my head.

"I didn't order…okay, I sort of did order them to help, but quite frankly, if you were doing *your* job I wouldn't have to."

"If—if I were doing my job?" Solair sputters but then visibly composes himself. "I have many irons in the fire, Varia. I don't have time to deal with every little thing."

"Every little thing like a decent place to sleep?" I frown up at him but try to keep my tone as civil as possible. Everyone in the mess hall is staring at us already and it makes me quite uncomfortable. "Can't you have some compassion? Most of these women aren't warriors, or even sailors, and all of them have been through trauma, some more than others. I'm no doctor, but I'll tell you right now that sleeping on the floor, even on a cushion, is terrible for your body."

I gesture toward the aft deck as his anger seems to drain out of his face.

"The bedding is just sitting there, on a soon-to-be derelict ship. Why wouldn't you collect it?"

I can see him wrestling with himself as he tries to decide if he still wants to be angry—even though he knows I'm right—about me bossing his men around. In the end, his reasonable side wins out, which makes my respect for him go up several notches.

Not that I trust him yet, of course.

While his eyes remain fixed on me, Solair opens his mouth and speaks in a voice loud enough to cut through the general murmur of the mess hall.

"Men." The Kilgari pause whatever they happened to be doing, forks hovering before mouths, feet hanging mid stride. "Our guests need decent bedding. Do I have any additional volunteers to go help the crew already stripping the hold of the *Frontier*?"

I'm both grateful and more than a little impressed when every single one of them raises their hands.

CHAPTER EIGHT

SOLAIR

I'll admit that it stung to give in to Varia's request, but I couldn't refute her logic. Besides, I'm not a bad sort. If I see an opportunity to make my unscheduled, possibly unwanted passengers more comfortable, of course I'll take it.

The Kilgari are not a warlike people. While we take steps to defend ourselves from other powers that are in the League of Non-Aligned Races, we do not go out and seek war. We've fought in some wars in our past prior to the founding of the League—notably against the Kraaj—but nothing in the scope of what the Ataxians and Alliance are doing to each other.

Those of our people who have displayed a desire to fight

have easily found ample opportunity to go over to the Ataxians or the Alliance to fight in their war.

But most Kilgari, like me, are not malicious or mean spirited.

What I don't take kindly to is the way this blasted woman just ordered my men about like they were under her own command. I also can't stand the way she turns everything into an argument. For fuck's sake, this is my ship! You'd think she'd realize I know a thing or two about running it.

But what I find really troubling isn't the way she continually challenges me. It's the fact that she looks so damn gorgeous doing so. Again, I fight down the urge to tell her she might be my mate. I'm not sure if I should be hopeful that she is… or hopeful that she is not.

As my men filter out of the mess hall to go and acquire bedding from the mostly scrapped IHC vessel, I turn back to Varia and arch my eyebrows.

"Does that assuage your concerns?"

"It's a start." She sighs, and I think she might be trying to at least sound a little less acerbic. "Look, Captain Solair—"

"You can address me as Solair, if you wish."

"Fine. Look, Solair, I'm grateful for your help with bedding and with rescuing us in the first place, but we're going to need more than a place to sleep.

"For one thing, we're all in desperate need of showers, and clean garments would be a blessing if you have laundry facilities on board."

My nose twitches, and I realize that the human women are rather rank. I had assumed at first that this was just the way their sapient species smells, but I'm relieved to find that it's not.

"That's not an unreasonable request. I'll have Kintar show your woman Marion where the sonic showers are. If you like, I'll post guards outside to make sure you don't get walked in on."

"That would be fantastic." She grimaces and sits down on a nearby bench.

"What's the matter? Are you ill?" I crouch down next to her, awkwardly trying to touch her and still be comforting at the same time. "Nicari can take a look at you, if need be."

"I'm fine." She waves off my concerns as she catches her breath. "I've just got a touch of cryo atrophy. On that subject... is there anywhere on your ship I can work out?"

"Work out?" I cock my head to the side. "You mean, work outside the ship's hull? I leave that to very experienced work crews, but I'm sure that if you want I can..."

"No, no, no." Varia sighs, her shoulders heaving, as she rubs a hand down her face. Her eyes peek over her hand, filled with barely contained frustration. "When I say work out, it's a human term for exercise."

"Oh." I consider her query for a time. "We do most of our training in the cargo hold because the space is ideal, but I'm certain we can find other arrangements for you and your outer working."

"Working out."

"That's what I said. If you'll follow me?"

I offer my hand to assist her to a standing position, but in spite of her physical infirmity she refuses to take it and stands on her own. I shrug and take my hand away, instead gesturing for her to come with me.

"Where are we going?"

"A seldom used cargo bay where we store nautical supplies, such as fishing tack."

"Fishing tack?"

"Yes. This ship used to belong to my father, and though I've never done so, it is capable of landing on large bodies of saltwater. It would be a simple matter to rearrange the bay to allow sufficient room for your purposes."

She nods, lips becoming a thin, tight line. We head out of the mess hall and into the sleek corridors of my ship. I think I'm beginning to understand this strange, fiery woman. Most of her chagrin is born from a desire to protect the people she has taken under her wing. I can't fault her for that.

But still, is she really my mate? I'd have to kiss her to be certain, and at the moment I think we're about a hundred years from that even being a possibility. One thing's for sure—Varia Dawn is going to do whatever Varia Dawn thinks is best—and a person can either help her or get out of her way. But she won't be convinced otherwise.

I can't decide if I find her infuriating or appealing... or perhaps both. Much like extreme cold can cause wounds similar to burns, her caustic nature and refusal to back down are something of an aphrodisiac.

"You said before that this is a merchant ship. What kind of cargo do you normally carry?"

I start, because I hadn't been expecting her to speak.

"Oh, it depends upon the season, our vector, and a lot of other details. We've hauled foodstuffs, machine parts, even weapons a few times, although I prefer to stay away from that kind of merchandise—not to mention those kinds of clients."

I leave out that sometimes we smuggle contraband because I don't want to give her more cause to be distrustful. It's not that I'm greedy; operating this old ship takes a lot of resources, and not every job pays out as good as you think it will. One time I arrived at dock with a cargo bay full of *kufula* fruit only to find that the vendor who was to purchase it had disappeared, leaving his shop shuttered and abandoned.

So yes, sometimes I skirt the law and carry more valuable, though high-risk, cargo on my ship. It keeps the operation going, my men happy, and their cred accounts at least a little filled.

But most of all, it lets me keep and maintain my family's ship. I'd sooner lose my own arm than the *Queen*.

We travel through the bowels of the ship, and I stop from time to time to speak with my crew. Mostly, they all know their jobs very well and they just want to touch base. Varia waits patiently while I take care of business and then we continue our walk.

"The cargo hold is up ahead." I gesture toward the smooth black bulk of the cargo hold door. "It's not terribly large, but I hope it suits your purposes well enough."

I press on the control panel next to the door, keenly aware of how closely Varia watches my every move. She's probably watching to learn how to open the door herself. That bothers me, though I know it should not.

The door recesses into the wall a bit and then slides to the left, revealing the cargo hold. The lights flicker on, at least some of them. Since we don't use this hold much, it's been neglected from a maintenance purview.

Varia walks inside, her eyes narrowed to slits and her

brow furrowed with thought. She turns in a slight circle, taking in the haphazardly piled equipment, dusty crates and barrels with chagrin written on her pretty face. She turns to me, arms akimbo, and I know I'm about to get another lambasting from her sharp tongue.

"This is where you expect me to exercise?" she scoffs, gesturing at the room with one hand. "Are you kidding me?"

"What's wrong with it?" I frown and glance about the room. "Not spacious enough?"

"It's plenty spacious. That's not the point."

"Then what is your point, Varia?"

She heaves an exasperated sigh—which does things to her chest that I find rather distracting—and slams her fist on a nearby crate, sending dust into the air.

"My point is all of this junk is in the way. Can't you find someone to move it?"

I grin ear to ear.

"Why, yes. I can find someone, and quickly."

"Good."

I point my finger at her and smile more widely. At first, she frowns in confusion, but then light dawns in her eyes and she bares her teeth in a snarl.

"You are such an asshole."

Varia turns away from me and grabs a nearby crate, dragging it across the room toward the far wall as sweat beads on her forehead.

She certainly is furious, but in a strange way I think I'm starting to like her anger.

CHAPTER NINE

VARIA

If I was trying to make a point, I didn't have to pull my shoulder out of socket to do it. This crate is about three times as heavy as I expected. Still, I can't let him see me sweat over the weight.

Shit. Too late. A droplet of sweat streaks from my eyebrow down to my cheek, and my only hope is that he was looking the other way when it happened. Unfortunately for me, he's leaning against the door frame with that infuriating, cursedly sexy smirk on his face.

"Enjoying yourself over there?" I can't help edging a little bit of snark into my voice. If he was any kind of male, he would be throwing his shoulders into this alongside me.

"I'm doing just fine, thanks."

If anything, he lazes even further into his slouch against the open portal, folding his arms across that broad chest. I don't mind admitting I'd welcome seeing him work up a sweat—even if it was just helping me lug these crates into something resembling order.

Once I've managed to scrape my burden squarely into one corner, I turn to face the rest of the dusty monuments scattered randomly through the dim room. God, I hope I started with the heavy one. There are one or two of comparable size, so I imagine the best strategy is to drag them over by this one and see if I can stack everything smaller on top of them.

One big pile is unsightly, but it's a damn sight better than having everything jumbled around. I have it halfway across the floor when wisdom crackles my way from the peanut gallery.

"You know, if I was you, I might use them to create barriers."

"What's that?"

"Figure out a floor plan and organize things so that the larger space can be partitioned into smaller ones. Create a bit of privacy."

He makes a fair point, but I rankle at it immediately.

"You look plenty strong, Solair. I'd welcome it any time you opted to help."

"I think I'll pass." Every inch of my skin crackles at his casual derision.

I glare and grunt at him. "Get over here and help me."

His easy smile vanishes, and he finally sidles away from his roost to stand squarely between me and the doorway. All the hairs on my arms stand up at once. It's a move that is mildly threatening and entirely thrilling.

"It's been a long time since I've been in the position of taking orders, Varia. As commander of this vessel, I've got more pressing duties to attend to than helping you set up house."

"What, like leaning against the wall ogling me?" He tenses at the baldness of my statement, but doesn't refute what I said.

"Like making sure we can support an occupancy that has nearly doubled in size. Thank the stars so many of your number are in cryo-stasis, but they still need to be attended. Things may not be entirely to your liking, but I have yet to hear a single word of gratitude out of you for my decision to save your ass."

I can't help being cowed by this. It's true, if it weren't for the arrival of the *Ancestral Queen*, I would likely be sitting in the dark right now, trying not to count the minutes until the inevitable.

"Now," he says, "I understand you need a place for your people to stay, but if you want to carve out room on my ship for an exercise arena, you're damn well going to have to work for it."

"You're sounding more heroic by the minute, Captain. It's a wonder I haven't thanked you a hundred times over," I mumble to myself.

"What's that?" He tips his head, the light of the hold glinting off his golden horns.

"You got us off of that ship and I should be grateful for that, but I don't relish the thought of being brought onto another ship to be treated as a toy or a slave. And that's the truth of it."

Solair's golden eyes blaze for a moment before narrowing under his thundering brows. His lips are pulled tightly and his chest heaves as sharp breaths rasp through his nostrils. Now I'm not the only one with sweat beading on their forehead.

A tiny flicker fires off somewhere deep in my core and I realize how completely alone we are. It's just the two of us standing inches from each other, deep in the disused bowels of this ship. This close, it's like I can feel his heart pounding between us. I can't tell if it's with rage, or the same curious proximity I'm feeling.

My defense slips, and something in my eyes betrays me. Whatever it is, Solair catches it immediately. The furrow in his brow relaxes and the gold shines in his eyes.

When he's not being impossible, he's not bad looking at all.

I wonder what he thinks about me?

Wait, where did that come from? As soon as the thought crops up, I send it whistling away. It's something I'm going to have to deal with later—when I'm not squared against him like some prize-fighter waiting to see where the punches will land.

He makes as if to say something, parting his lips and inhaling before clamping his mouth shut again. Temptation riffles through me. Given how little I've wanted to hear him chortling away, goading me to work, I would desperately like to know what he was about to say.

A sensation I'm unfamiliar with bubbles up between my ribs. Is it shame? Embarrassment?

Sure, Solair hasn't exactly been rolling out the red carpet for us, but he did pull us out of danger. And at no small inconvenience to himself and his crew. He hasn't been making it easy, but he has been helping us. Helping *me*.

Suddenly, the dim, dusty room afforded me seems like a precious gift. Is it ideal? No, but it's a far cry from the stifling uncertainty I sweltered in a scant few hours ago.

My eyes have drifted from his to take in the space around us, and when they find his again, the beast that had been boiling under his skin seems to have fled. He's completely changed, stilled. Somewhere between gentle and composed.

"It's been an exhausting day for everyone," his voice is subdued and oddly distant, "maybe you should rest before trying to wrestle all this into shape." He gives a loose shrug to the detritus strewn about us.

I make to answer, but this time I come up short of words. My mouth is dry and sticky. What's wrong with me?

Solair leans in again, as if to catch whatever words fall out of my mouth. Is that what I looked like? Expectant, almost imploring?

My head swims at the moment and I just nod a couple of times before gliding past him into the corridor. My body feels detached from my mind. Not that my mind is doing much. Everything feels cloudy and heavy.

I'm hungry. That must be it. For all the time I spent in the mess earlier, I seem to have digested it all and am hungry again.

Maybe my body is just trying to make up from having to starve for the last week.

We've been subsisting on bare rations for days and I've expended more energy than is remotely wise. He's right. I should eat something and put my head down for a while before I try conquering any other monsters. Even if the monsters are my own.

Once I've gotten a little something in my stomach, I'll try and get some sleep. Who knows when I last managed to cobble together more than a few minutes of sleep?

It would be nice to chalk up my irritability to weariness and hunger, but I worry it could be something more. When we were all huddled against the inevitable on the *Frontier*, I had a purpose. While I hate to admit it, I thrive on the command. Now that we've been pulled out of that hole, we've been thrown into chaos and I don't have any clear footing.

There's an established hierarchy on the *Ancestral Queen*, and it doesn't include me in any leadership capacity. I'm just one more "rescued woman," and that's a pretty disempowered place to be. The last thing in the universe I want to be is just another victim waiting to be saved by the "big strong alien." I'm more than that.

I don't hear Solair tromping along behind me and, for whatever reason, I can't bring myself to look back. It's hard to say why. Maybe I would be comforted by the sight of that broad-shouldered man lumbering after me. Maybe a tiny part of me cherishes the sensation of being saved.

CHAPTER TEN

Solair

My boots clank loudly on the deck plating as I exit the cargo hold, my stride as swift as it is stiff. Before the *Queen* ran into the *Frontier's* floating bulk in the abyss of space, I could count the number of times I was frustrated on zero fingers.

That's not exactly true, but I'd become so accustomed to the cadence and flow of life aboard a privateer ship, I guess I learned to take everything in stride. We don't have enough fuel to make it to the edge of the Badlands? No problem, I can work with that. The client is refusing to pay our full commission because of some asinine reason? I can deal with that, too.

I can even handle my crew's constantly shifting demands,

usually for more money or a bigger take. It's a common fallacy that the captain is unquestionably in command with no oversight from his crew. That only happens on military ships. On a privateer ship like the *Ancestral Queen*, I only command so long as my crew allows.

Sure, I could kick them off my ship, but I can't hope to work a vessel this size by myself. So even though I have that option on paper, I don't really have that possibility.

But I can deal with all their various anxieties and personal melodramas. It's part of being a captain. It's not all dashing and daring do. A whole lot of the job entails making people feel better, both about themselves and the mission.

Someone would think with all of that experience, I could deal with one, admittedly combative human female. But this has proven to be one of the most daunting challenges I've ever engaged.

Maybe if I had it to do over again, I would just turn around and leave the *Frontier* to rot. But even as I think it, I realize that, too, is not an option. I wouldn't have been able to live with myself if I'd condemned so many women to a slow, agonizing death.

So, the survivors from the *Frontier* have now been added to the stack of burdens on my shoulders. And I could probably manage that a lot better if not for their fiery tempered de facto leader, Varia.

Her face when she realized I wasn't going to help her move all the cargo out of the way so she could have her exercise room... If looks could kill, I would be a dead male. But from my perspective, I'm already bending over backward to accommodate the survivors. Does she have any idea the chaos caused by the mere presence of females on a Kilgari ship? No one knows quite how to act. We're all used to taking orders from women, so our default has been to give them pretty much whatever they desire if it's within reason.

Though to be honest... the Kilgari matriarchal tradition isn't really what has me tense and confused about Varia. Not at all. The first time I laid eyes upon her, I was struck with both her strength and her beauty. Here was a woman with next to no resources and still she managed to save dozens of lives.

Of course I noticed her physical attractiveness right away. But then she opened her mouth and snapped out icy daggers of demanding words, which had been tipped with acid. I find she's perhaps the single most infuriating being in the galaxy.

It's as if she was schooled on how to annoy me, and not only did she have perfect attendance but blew the grade curve. Or perhaps she can psionically see into my mind and pick out the best ways to drive me absolutely crazy?

When I was a child, and this ship belonged to my father, he told me of how Kilgari males innately sensed their mates. He claimed I would know the truth of it beyond a shadow of a doubt. He also said that my mate would complement me perfectly.

These teachings were written in the Elder Scrolls of our people, transcribed from the lessons of the Precursors who gave life to the Kilgar and visited their earliest creations from time to time.

Imagine my surprise when the I first laid eyes upon Varia, breathed her scent, and felt as if she were destined to be my mate. A human woman would seem utterly absurd as my ideal mate, but here we are.

But as I mentioned before, she started talking, and to say that she does not complement me at all is an understatement. Quite the opposite, it's as if she's constantly firing the starboard engines while I insist on using the port side. I'm going around in circles, and I don't like the feeling one bit.

In our society today, it's almost unheard of for a Kilgari to find their destined mate. With so few females to go around, it comes down to personal choice and a willingness to be the fifth or sixth husband to one of the matriarchs.

So really, I have no frame of reference to know if what I feel is the certainty of destiny. I can only guess and assume. But I will say that even if she is utterly infuriating, I can't get Varia out of my mind.

This makes me wonder if maybe she really is my destined mate. If so, it muddles things more than ever before because it's not panning out the way my father said it would. Not one bit. There's currently no indication that Varia and I will evolve into a harmonious dynamic, other than my gut instinct.

But over the years of commanding the *Ancestral Queen*, I've learned to trust my gut as much, or even more than, my sensor array. Sure, the console on the bridge can tell me the ship's speed, possible crew complement and active weapons arrays, but only my gut gives me any inkling if they're friend or foe.

My gut is telling me that mine and Varia's destinies are intertwined, tangled like forest vines so badly it's hard to tell where she ends and I begin. But what will all of this even mean to her if I'm right?

I find that I've wandered up to the bridge. Due to the informality of my ship, no one leaps up to snap off a crisp salute. My yeoman does mutter out a halfhearted "captain on the bridge" for the unwary, but by and large everyone knows their jobs and I don't see a need to meddle.

Stepping up to my command console, I sit and punch a few keys. The first thing I want to check on is the progress of stripping the IHC *Frontier* ship. From the looks of my monitor, it's going quite well, but at the moment Kintar and the human woman Marion are engaged in a heated argument. I dial up the volume so I can hear them speak.

"...for the last time, we only have enough sanitation tissue to provide one roll per quarters. You'll just have to ration them." Kintar's tone is patient, but I can see the way a big vein in his temple twitches, just below his sawed-off horns.

"Ration toilet paper?" Marion sighs, and puts her arms akimbo as she glares up at my quartermaster. "You do realize that women need to use it for more than one place, yes?"

Kintar is a seasoned warrior, though he's given up that path, and he doesn't shake easily. But I can't stop a smile from stretching over my lips at the sight of him feeling so uncomfortable.

"Well, perhaps... perhaps I can spare a few more."

"Now you're speaking my language, big guy."

I've heard enough. I turn off the monitor and lean back in my chair, rubbing the base of my horns. While the salvage operation seems to be going well, any fool can see that sooner or later we're going to have to find more space for our new—what should I call them? Guests? Refugees? Certainly, they aren't crew, but then again given the way so many of them try to just take over, I might want to rethink that notion.

I go over a few ideas in my head, but I know better than to implement any of them without Varia's consent and tacit approval. I might be dense at times, but I eventually learn.

So, I rise from my command chair and head off the bridge, my head full of troubles. Despite what may or may not be going on between me and Varia, she is her people's leader. I'll need her involvement if I'm to locate more suitable space for them.

I just hope we can come to an agreement without shouting at each other.

CHAPTER ELEVEN

VARIA

The walls of our makeshift bunk space curve upward toward the ceiling, the burnished copper color a less than ideal but functional mirror reflecting the images of myself, Thrase, and Lamira as we play a few hands of Twonk on my bunk.

My best friend's wide mouth stretches in a grin, and she lays down her hand on the rumpled blanket. "Three Commanders, two Priestesses. Read it and weep."

Thrase pushes her glasses up further on her nose and peers intently at the cards. "Why did you call the Companion a Priestess?"

I chuckle and arrange the cards in my hand. "Because

Lamira learned to play Twonk with Solaris refugees from the Ataxian Coalition. The Ataxians replace the Companion card with a Priestess."

"Hmph." Thrase straightens her posture and looks at the cards in her hand with disgust. "Figures the Flame Lickers would obfuscate even card games."

"According to the Ataxians, they invented Twonk and the Trident Alliance copied it."

Thrase's brows raise on her forehead as she arranges her cards. "It wouldn't be the first time someone else took credit for another's accomplishments. Did I ever tell you about the time that my professor..."

"Stole your research and then claimed you were obsessed with him romantically?" I chuckle. "Only about a dozen times since we woke on the *Frontier*."

"Well, it still stings." Thrase slaps her cards down on the bed and throws up her hands. "I don't know why I keep arranging my cards when they're going to suck no matter what."

Their gazes snap over to me in unison.

"It's time to put up or shut up, missy." Lamira's eyes gleam with lust. In lieu of creds, we're betting the thin, crispy dessert rounds that Jax baked in droves. Most of the women from the *Frontier* are already fighting over them, but this way seemed more egalitarian.

"If you insist..." I lay my cards down, revealing that I have four Lieutenants, one from each suit. "Four of a kind trumps three of a kind."

"Oh, get stuffed." Lamira's grin belies her harsh words. "Probably cheating."

Thrase purses her lips and considers the pile of cookies. "I don't know, I think it may have been sheer skill..."

I gather up my cookies protectively in my embrace and glare at them in mock avarice. "Stop sucking up. You're not getting any."

Despite my words, I wind up doling out some of the crisps to my roommates. Sighing, I reach up and vigorously scratch my scalp. I swear it feels like I dipped my head in a vat of engine grease.

"Still waiting on your turn for a shower?"

I glance over at Lamira and nod. "Solair's people have been very accommodating, but there was still a waiting list a mile long."

"And being the selfless leader you are, you put yourself at the bottom." Lamira shakes her head, letting her dark hair fall out over her slender shoulders. "But selfish little me has already had a shower, and let me tell you, it was glorious."

"Ha ha ha. Laugh it up, bestie. See if you get any more of my cookies."

Thrase swings her legs over the edge of the bed and kicks her bare feet almost like a child. "Varia, the other women have been talking, and the general consensus is that we all want to return to IHC space."

I purse my lips and frown at this tidbit of information. Considering many of the women who were on the *Frontier* are criminals, I'm surprised they want to do any such thing. Then again, there is something to the old adage of the devil you know...

"I still can't fathom why I ended up being arrested in the first place." Thrase shakes her head. "All the research I was doing was completely legal. I don't even cheat on my IHC tax forms."

I nod and gesture toward my best friend. "Lamira never did anything wrong, either, but she was arrested just the same."

"Yeah." Lamira nods sagely. "You didn't do anything wrong either. Did you, Varia?"

"Ah..." I don't want to out and out lie to my best friend, but at the same time I'd hate to have her learn of my somewhat checkered past. I'm not saying I deserved to be shoved into a cryopod and shipped halfway across the galaxy, but I am saying my arrest didn't come as much of a surprise. "I think the more important question is *why* we were all incarcerated and put on that ship, not how."

Thrase nods, her eyes shining behind her spectacles. "It is

a mystery. Isn't it? I do love intrigue, whether I find it with a microscope or with my naked eyes."

Our makeshift bunk house was never meant to function as quarters, so there's no door chime. Instead someone pounds on the metal exit with their fist.

"Come in."

A Kilgari pushes the door open, his eyes nervously avoiding all of our gazes. "I was directed to tell you the shower is ready for you, Varia."

"Oh thank god. I'm about to scratch a hole in myself over here." I rise from the bed and follow the Kilgari out of the room. At the door, I stop and turn to jab my finger accusingly at the two women. "Don't touch my cookies."

Jax is an excellent cook. I guess I had no idea how much a good meal would change my mood. If only the captain was as easy to get along with as the ship's chef.

The Kilgari crewman leads me toward the aft deck, where the sonic showers are located. I step into the chamber and am struck immediately by the artistic flares. Each sonic emitter has been sculpted to resemble a piscine creature with its mouth open. They sort of look like dolphins from Earth, except for their razor-sharp teeth and frills around their necks. The tiles themselves are done in a crisscrossing blue and white pattern that reminds me of shallow tropical waters.

The *Ancestral Queen* is an old enough ship that such aesthetics were still considered integral to the overall design—as vital as life support. These days, both the Alliance and the IHC make boring boxy ships, with no thought to aesthetics at all. At least the Ataxians still like to get artistic with their designs.

But the Kilgari—they build not just ships, but works of art.

One advantage of a sonic shower is that if you hang your garments under the spigot you can give them a quick cleanup without having to wait hours for them to dry. I do just that before stepping under one of the free emitters and turning it on. There's only the slightest buzz as the solid sound molecules gently scrub the detritus and grease from my skin. It's not as nice as a water shower, but in space fresh water is too valuable a resource to waste it cleaning.

My clothes and skin are scrubbed, but my garments have that tinny sort of ozone smell that comes with sonic cleaning. Oh well, it's better than putting dirty clothes onto my clean body.

When I exit the shower, I inform the Kilgari that I can make it back on my own, mostly because I want a little time to think. I find it hard to fathom why so many of the women want to return to the IHC when they'll be facing criminal charges. I'm willing to return and face the music, so to speak, but my motivations are out of helping Lamira clear her name rather than fleeing toward something familiar.

I gently rap on the door to our chamber, but I hear no response. One press of the button later the door slides open with a soft hiss, and I look in on the darkened chamber. My roommates are already asleep.

Gratefully lying down into my first night of non-itchy rest in some time, my mind won't let me find slumber easily. It whirls with the tumultuous events of the past few days, from our hardscrabble quest for survival to the unexpected rescue by Solair and his men.

And there's still so much to take care of. We need to finish salvaging anything useful off the *Frontier*, not to mention carefully moving those cryopods still actively containing women.

There's no way I can trust Big Gold to take care of it all himself. Not at this point in my life. I've lived too long and experienced too much incompetence to trust anyone else to handle matters of importance. Unless I think they can do a better job, which hasn't happened yet.

It's the last thing on my mind before I finally drift off to sleep.

CHAPTER TWELVE

SOLAIR

As we get to Delta shift, the normally busy bridge becomes a fortress of solitude for me. I'm glad for the solace and the silence because my mind whirls with problems and potential solutions.

First and foremost, I've decided beyond a shadow of a doubt that Varia and the other refugees we found on the *Frontier* need to go. Period. Is it nice having women around, especially for a Kilgari? Of course it is.

But at the same time, women on a Kilgari ship are nothing but disruptive. The refugees have proven this much already. And I can't fault them one bit because our own nature is at the root of our problems.

Kilgari society honors and reveres females to the point of near total devotion. It's just not in our nature to say no to a woman. With all of my men fighting their instincts to defer to the women—even to the point of contradicting their own captain's orders—I can see nothing but trouble ahead for the *Ancestral Queen*.

So, for no fault of their own, and not even a fault of ours, we need to find a place to dump... that is, a place to *relocate* Varia and her fellow survivors. And I have more than just the obvious reasons for doing so.

When we came across the *Frontier*, I was more greedy than curious. After all, finding a derelict IHC ship in Kilgari territory is almost unheard of. But then we boarded the decrepit vessel and found all the crew dead. The only place with anyone living was the reinforced hold that Varia and her followers jury rigged into a life pod.

Which begs the question, who sent the distress call if all of the crew were dead? And we still haven't solved the mystery of why one hundred and seven women were drifting in a decrepit hulk in the first place.

No doubt about it, Varia and her followers are going to bring trouble, more than they already have. Sooner or later whoever canned them up on that floating coffin is going to come looking, and this is hardly a vessel of war. Sure, we're not defenseless, but the *Queen's* main purpose is moving cargo and looking damn good while she does it.

In a protracted fire fight against tough opposition, I'm not confident enough in our chances to take the risk.

I press keys on my console and bring up the local star system maps. Some habitable worlds are a relatively short superluminal jump away, but they lack any form of advanced civilization. I'd be marooning the women on the surface, which is not the sort of decision I can make with a clear conscience.

Rubbing the bridge of my nose, I sigh, head dipped and horns drooping toward the console. Things were running so smoothly before one hundred and seven women floated into our lives.

But all hope is not lost. All I have to do is find a decent place to leave Varia and the others, and things will quickly go back to the way they were before. There's a comfort, a solace in that, which can't be measured.

Stagnation be damned, I want my ship back to the way it was, with plenty of cargo space, no need to worry about life support, and a crew bereft of feminine distractions.

Part of me wonders if any of the other Kilgari have felt the same thing I have of it it's in my imagination, namely that one of the one hundred and seven is their fated mate. It's not like I have such deep conversations with my crew, not about that subject at least. There's sort of an unspoken agreement among a Kilgari crew that when it comes to women, it's best not to bring the subject up at all. It will make people anxious at best and downright illogical at worst.

I'm still no closer to figuring out an answer. For the time being, the women are here and must be dealt with. I can decide what to do with them on the morrow.

Overall, we're not doing badly in terms of supplies, even with the additional passengers, but there's no harm in playing it safe.

I have nothing left to do now but to head for my cabin and take a much-needed rest. Rubbing my eyes, I unfold from my command seat and head for the bridge exit.

When the alarm klaxon sounds, I actually laugh because I can't believe it's for real. There must have been some sort of malfunction. But I head for my console and bring up the alarm display. The sensors have detected a nearby ship with its "spoilsport" active—the slang term for auto destruct.

In a panic, I assume it must be the worst-case scenario, namely the *Frontier*. If that ship goes up, the shockwave could cause damage to the *Ancestral Queen*.

My fingers dance over the keys, attempting to open a comm channel to the shuttle's bridge, but I'm met with repeated failure. Either someone is jamming my transmission—which seems highly unlikely—or the transport vessel's comms are down.

But I have other methods of seeing what occurs on the other ship. I patch in my command console to the security monitors on the transport, and then gape in astonishment as I see Ilya and Swipt scrambling about on the bridge. Judging from the frantic way they jam their fingers on the various consoles, they're well aware of the auto destruct being activated and are engaged in trying to stop it.

I've not lasted this long as captain by relying upon assumptions, however. Using my console, I dial up the specific frequency used by my first mate, Grantian.

"Solair to Grantian, come in."

There's a brief pause, and then I hear his weary voice over the line.

"What's up, Cap?"

"Trouble. I need you to grab a portable short comm and rush to the aft deck. You should be able to get a signal to the *Frontier* bridge."

"Why am I doing this again?"

"Because that ship has just engaged its auto destruct sequence, and I can't get through to Swipt."

"Acknowledged. Grantian out."

At times like these the command chair can feel like a prison. Every instinct makes me want to rush about and try to fix this personally, but that's not my place. They say that while the captain's seat is the biggest, you'll find no rest there. I think I can appreciate that on a new level right now.

The minutes tick by, and I drum my fingers on the console in frustration. I just have to be patient. Grantian is a good man, ostensibly my best. He used to work for a mercenary unit, the famed Kell Hounds, so I know I can rely upon him in an emergency like this one.

I nearly faint with relief when the comm crackles to life and I hear Grantian's voice.

"We've got major problems, Captain. The *Frontier's* auto destruct sequence is locked in, and neither Swipt nor the human woman can figure out how to unlock it."

Damn. My hands tighten into fists at my sides.

"How much time do we have?"

"Less than ten minutes."

Ten minutes? I do the calculations in my head, but there's no time to get the remaining cryostasis pods off the *Frontier*. I don't even bother thinking about the salvage operation because it doesn't seem important when compared to the potential lives lost.

Saving the *Ancestral Queen* is simple, even easy. All I have to do is decouple our linked ships and pilot us to a safe distance. But that decision will condemn not only my pilot and the Ilya woman to death, but all of those poor souls still locked in cryostasis.

My mind locks up, and I fight down a wave of panic.

What should I do? What can I do? Someone is going to die no matter what.

And as captain, it will all be my fault.

CHAPTER THIRTEEN

Varia

My eyes snap open the instant the alarm klaxon sounds. As a testament to my military training, I've got the covers flung back and am halfway dressed before my roommates have awakened fully.

"Varia?" Lamira rubs sleep out of her eyes, a line of drool decorating her chin. "What's going on? Why is the alarm sounding?"

"I don't know, but I mean to find out. Stay here. Stay safe."

"Maybe I can help." Thrase slips into an oversized shirt borrowed from one of the Kilgari and rises to her bare feet.

I start to argue with her, but Thrase has at least three

PhDs that I know of. Maybe she can help. "All right. Can you gather as many of the *Frontier* girls together in the cargo bay as possible? I've a feeling we might want to all be together in case something happens."

"I'll do my best."

With that, I leave my borrowed quarters and rush out into dimly lit corridor. Given that it's a sleep cycle, the illumination is low, but the flashing warning lights more than compensate for the lack of light.

The *Queen* isn't a capital class ship, but it still seems to take an eternity to race up from my quarters to the bridge. I dance from foot to foot while waiting for the automatic door to hiss open before I race inside.

I spot Solair right away, moving about from console to console and constantly barking orders over comms.

"Montier, make sure that all maintenance cycles are turned off. I want the *Queen* ready for subluminal transit yesterday."

"Copy that."

I move over next to Solair and lean on the console while he angrily pecks at the keys. "What's going on?"

He doesn't even look at me. Instead, he completely ignores me and continues to move around the bridge like a jumping beetle on caffeine.

"All emergency crews report to stations. This is not a drill. I repeat, this is not a drill."

"Hey." I wave my hand at him, but he continues to dance about the bridge without even so much as a glance in my direction. "Goddamn it, Solair, I'm talking to you."

Now his gaze does flick over to mine, but only for an instant before he gets back on the comm. It lasts long enough for me to catch the clear irritation in his golden eyes.

"Nicari, prepare med bay for potential casualties..."

I step right in front of him, and he tries to sidle past me, but I keep moving every time he moves. At length Solair gives up on his tactic of ignoring me and shouts in exasperation. "Will you please move the fuck out of my way?"

"As soon as you tell me what the fuck is going on."

Solair grimaces, and his golden-eyed gaze glances over at the nearby console. "The *Frontier*, for reasons unknown, has activated its spoilsport."

"Spoilsport?"

"Self-destruct sequence."

He moves around me as I stand frozen in shock. The *Frontier* is going to self-destruct?

"But what about all of the women still in cryopods?" I

dance after him as he moves from console to console belting out orders. "Solair, you have to save them. You have to."

Solair turns toward me, his jowls quivering in barely contained anger.

"What do you think I'm trying to do?"

My mouth closes, and I step out of his way. It's obvious that my presence is a hindrance to Solair, so I rush out of the bridge and head for the cargo bay at a dead run. Cursing my cryo atrophy, I struggle to keep my legs pumping, drawing in one agonized breath after another into my tortured lungs until I reach the bowels of the ship. When I arrive, more than half of the survivors from the *Frontier* are waiting for me along with at least that many Kilgari. Everyone seems to be waiting for someone else to take charge.

I rush up next to Marion and lean on her for support until I manage to catch my wind enough for stunted speech.

"We need to... get the cryopods... off the *Frontier*... eight minutes left."

Her eyes widen with understanding and she turns around to organize everyone into groups. The Kilgari are not dumb. Once they realize what our purpose is, they leap right into the fray to offer their assistance.

Cryopods weigh over five hundred pounds on a good day,

but the two different groups manage to coordinate their efforts with aplomb. Of course, it takes one Kilgari on a cryopod side while it takes four of us to lift the other end, but we make it work.

I join in the effort, rushing over to the dying ship and helping to pick up a pod. Our feet slide about on the metal deck plating as we struggle with our heavy burden until a couple of Solair's men join us. I'm a little bit miffed by how much difference their strength makes, though I know that's silly.

When I return to the cargo bay of the *Ancestral Queen*, I find that Marion and Kintar have appropriated some hover platforms to facilitate the removal of the cryopods. Now we can move them as fast as our feet will shuffle between the ships, which turns out to be pretty quick.

"Come on. Hurry." We rush over to the *Frontier* and load another pod onto the working sled. "Come on, come on, come on."

Lamira grimaces at me from across the sled. "You know, saying that doesn't make us move any faster."

"Maybe not, but it makes me feel better."

She laughs, though the tension doesn't leave her eyes. I thought I told her to wait in our quarters. How am I supposed to keep her safe if she won't listen to me?

No time to argue over it now. There's no time at all.

As we reenter the *Ancestral Queen's* hold, we nearly run into another hover sled crew.

"This is the last of them." I wave them out of our way and I check my chronometer. My heart jumps into my throat when I see that we have under two minutes left before the *Frontier* blows to kingdom come.

"Seal the hatch, uncouple the IHC ship." One of the Kilgari moves over to do just that, but Kintar grabs him by the arm.

"Stop, you fool. We still have people over there."

"But we're all going to die if I don't. Tough luck for them, but there's no point in all of us getting killed."

Kintar glares at his fellow Kilgari until the crewman wilts. He stares into the darkness of the *Frontier* through the coupling, his jaw set hard. Despite his bravado, I know he means to do exactly what the crewman had intended if he thinks there's no other choice.

But then the sound of rapid footfalls reaches our ears, and I peer intently through the aperture. The running forms of Gratian, Ilya, and Swipt come into view, the danger written on their terrified faces.

"Out of the way, move." Swipt rushes past us and heads out of the cargo bay, presumably heading for the *Ancestral Queen's* bridge. I notice Ilya is in hot pursuit, but there's no time to think about that at the moment.

In surprisingly short order—I envy his long legs—Swipt's voice comes over the general hail, a note of urgency in his normally laconic delivery.

"Everyone, Kilgari and human, find a place to strap in. It's about to get bumpy."

Kintar decouples the *Frontier*, and the whole ship lurches as the hulk drifts away from us slowly. Then we're nearly thrown off our feet as the main thruster array burns into life. I throw an arm up over my face to protect my vision from the sudden glare and drag Lamira down between the bulkhead and a cooling junction, the best crash seats I can find in a pinch.

The *Frontier* slowly lists, dwindling in the distance, until it suddenly evaporates into a globe of fire and an ever-expanding debris field. Lamira and I are thrown against the cooling unit with bruising force, but we manage to avoid serious injury as the shockwave hits the aft deck of the *Ancestral Queen*.

For a moment it seems like the expanding globe of plasma is going to envelop us, but gradually the *Queen* pulls away as its velocity increases. Swipt got us moving just in the nick of time.

But as I watch the *Frontier* disintegrate into so much flotsam and jetsam, I can't help but feel like there's a sinister hand at work here, destroying an evidence of why we were captured in the first place.

CHAPTER FOURTEEN

SOLAIR

All I wanted was to grab some shuteye before another day of trying to manage this fucked-up situation. That's it. Just a few quiet, Varia-free moments to myself. Even if she might be my fated mate, her persistence for me to aid her —and her insistence that I'm not doing enough—is taxing me to exhaustion.

And then—*then!*—the damn *Frontier* exploded. For no apparent reason. So instead of getting the sleep I so badly need and desire, I'm back up on the bridge of the *Queen* trying to figure out what the hell I'm supposed to do next, my head pounding so hard it feels like my horns are about to fall out.

Instead of retreating to her bunk to sleep—or whatever

else she does when she's not driving me absolutely crazy —Varia is installed on the bridge, raging over the destruction of the *Frontier*. Understandably, she's concerned and confused about what happened. I'm annoyed too since we were still in the process of offloading all the cargo I'd planned to use or sell. Everything that remained on board—including the bodies of the deceased crew—are now no more than space junk. Just another frustration added to the ever-growing pile.

And here I was thinking I'd found myself a jackpot. Fuck, was I wrong.

Varia, though, is pissed because that ship was the only means she and the other women had of figuring out why they'd all been captured. I know she'd planned to scour it from bow to stern once we'd finished clearing it out, believing that somewhere on the massive, floating tomb she'd find an answer to the question of why she'd been detained. Now that hope is no longer and she's completely losing herself, just as I would be.

What I wouldn't be, however, is taking it out on everyone around me, and especially not on those who've been doing their best to help my cause. With every moment that passes, I get closer to losing my temper. I have no idea how I've been able to keep my anger contained this long.

The last straw is when she snaps at Montier. I overhear her questioning his methods of searching the *Frontier's* logs, whether he'd done something to set off the self-destruct sequence, and that's it. I've had it. She may be beautiful, and I know she's trying to do best by "her girls," but she has no right to question the intentions of my crew. Especially not when they're bending over backward to do everything they can to help.

Montier stares at me from his seat in front of our own computer system, trying to tune out her tirade. I approach Varia on swift feet, stop abruptly before I run her down, and lace my fingers around her arm. At the feel of my skin on hers she whips her head in my direction, long hair splaying out around her in an arc. Her distracting scent assaults my nostrils, but I put a damper on my primal urges.

"A word, please?"

It sounds like a question, but my voice is laced with the authority of command. As she's had military experience, I know she won't mistake the tone. She only nods in answer, cheeks flushed with anger, and allows me to lead her away from where Montier and Swipt are trying hard not to look like they desperately want to eavesdrop.

I take her off the bridge altogether. The airlock hisses as the doors close behind us, and before she can even think about opening her mouth I detonate.

"I'd like to know who exactly you think you are, speaking to my crew like that. You're more insane than I originally thought if you think Montier had anything to do with the loss of that ship. He was given an order, by me, his captain, to recon the ship's logs to find out something—anything!—about why you and the other women now aboard this vessel were taken by the IHC. We're a tight crew and I trust my men completely. If I give them an order, they do it. He would never sabotage me and for you to insinuate that—"

She attempts to cut me off but I barrel on, completely steamrolling her efforts.

"I understand you're frustrated. I can't imagine what you and the others have gone through and are continuing to go through. If you haven't noticed, I didn't ask for this situation to happen either. I didn't set out to become a babysitter for a bunch of women. All I wanted to do was salvage a dead vessel. I have deliveries to make and you and your friends are completely screwing my timelines. Now, if you don't mind, I'd appreciate it if you'd remove yourself from my sight immediately before I actually say something I regret," I finish, not caring for a second how my words make her feel.

I'm the commander of this ship, not Varia Dawn. The sooner she realizes that, the easier her time here will be.

She stares at me for what feels like forever. The silence stretches endlessly between us, fraught with tension like intracloud lightning. It almost crackles in the air. Her eyes remain fixed on mine, but she doesn't say a word.

I continue to hold her gaze, waiting for her to react. She hasn't backed down from an argument yet, so I fully expect a snide comment or a quick, scathing retort, but it never comes. Instead, I watch her deflate, all her pugnacious bravado dissipating completely.

"You're right, Solair. I apologize," she says.

Her shoulders are rounded, and she appears cowed. Reticent. Fully and completely chastised. I'm shocked. In my wildest dreams I never would have thought she could appear so withdrawn. It's as if her entire, fiery essence has deserted her.

It makes me feel awful. I should know better. No one on this ship is without stress. As the leaders of our two factions, she and I bear the brunt of it. We should be working together, not against one another. We—*I*—need to try harder.

"No. I should apologize to you, Varia. That was—what I said was unnecessary. You're just trying to look after your people. You've suffered a grave violation and it's not fair of me to expect you to not be angry. You have every right to be upset," I tell her.

I can tell my words have shocked her. She stares up at me, those gorgeous, molten eyes wide, mouth ajar. The urge to kiss her and confirm the mating bond is fierce, but I keep hold of myself.

Silence settles between us once more, but this time it's

more comfortable. All I can hear is her breath, passing calmly in and out of her lungs, as if the softness in my tone was exactly what she needed to hear.

"May I ask a favor of you? Just one," she asks, finally finding her voice.

"Of course," I answer.

"I'd be grateful if you'd appoint some of your crew to assist me and my team with clearing the hold and improving our living quarters. They know this ship better than we do and I don't want to create more of a hassle for any of you," she says.

"I'll do that. I'll send some of my men to aid you tomorrow," I agree.

"Thank you."

Before I can say another word, she turns on her heel and takes off in the direction of her sleeping quarters, leaving me dumbfounded and alone with my thoughts. I watch her go, my eyes following her retreating form until it disappears completely from view.

How I wish this entire situation was different. If we'd met under any other circumstances, I could work on developing a traditional mating relationship with her. I could take my time and woo her and make her fall for me. I'd reveal the mating bond and she'd be happy for it.

CELIA KYLE & ATHENA STORM

There'd be nothing standing in the way of us being together, not like there is now.

Everything is so tense between us. We're nearly always at each other's throats, always battling one another for command with neither willing to concede. The constant power struggle is debilitating, like it's ruining us before there is an "us." I hate how we can't just talk to one another without dissolving into an argument. I'd kill to be able to have a normal conversation with her about anything other than this crazy situation we've found ourselves in.

But what's the point? She's made it abundantly clear that this arrangement is temporary; she doesn't want to stay here and plans to jump ship as soon as she's able. I don't know her very well, but I know nothing in the galaxy can convince her to do something she doesn't want. Mate or not, if she doesn't want to stay, there's no point in wasting my breath trying to convince her.

Once she's gone, I waste no time returning to the bridge. Swipt and Montier know better than to question me. In silence, we continue our journey through the stars.

CHAPTER FIFTEEN

VARIA

I've given up on seeing certain things during my lifetime. Peace between the Trident Alliance and the Ataxian Coalition. No radiation fusion reactors. Cute clothes with pockets.

I'd given up on any sort of true civility out of Solair, as well. But then he surprised me, apologizing for his rudeness and abrasive nature. Of course, he's feeling a bit resentful about the massive disruption to his normal routine. I get that. But it's not like any of us from the *Frontier* chose to be dropped on his doorstep.

Not only that, but once Solair figured out what was occurring on the *Frontier*, he could have turned his ship around and flown away into the event horizon. But he chose not to. He took responsibility, which was the moral thing to do, and now he's just going to have to learn to deal with the consequences.

As I sit on my bunk and stare at the concave burnished walls, I consider our most recent interaction to have gone well, all things considered. But he had been angry at first. Very, very angry.

I confess to feeling a stab of guilt when he pointed out we're keeping the *Ancestral Queen* from making her appointed rounds. He has deliveries to make, and I know enough about how privateer ships operate to know that if he doesn't deliver, he doesn't get paid. That trickles down to his men as well, which causes all of the problems someone might expect.

He is justified in feeling resentment and frustration, but not in how he expressed it. There was a moment there when his eyes were full of fury, his lips peeled back in a snarl, that I thought Solair would lock me up in his brig— if he even has one—and throw away the key.

But then his gaze softened and he'd apologized, which I feel in my heart was genuine.

And to be honest... I'm not the easiest person to deal with. I don't handle frustrations in stride like Marion, I'm not brilliant like Thrase, and not everyone likes me like Lamira. Due to my admittedly hardscrabble upbringing, I don't deal with change or frustration very well. I tend to be rude, blunt, and focused on fixing whatever problem I perceive, anyone else's feelings be damned.

But doesn't that put me just as much in the wrong as the Kilgari captain?

I'm still mulling over this latest dilemma when the door slides open and Lamira enters our room. "Hey, there. Why the long face?"

"The Kilgari captain and I had a bit of a fight."

Her reaction is less than impressive. "Again? That's hardly news. The whole ship is talking about all the heat between the two of you."

"Heat?" My cheeks flush, and in spite of myself an image of a naked, two-membered Solair pops into my head. "What in the world are you talking about? Who's saying that? I'm not into alien guys, not at all."

"What am *I* talking about? What are *you* talking about?" Lamira laughs hard at my expense. "I meant 'heat' as in you guys don't seem to get along. You're the one who's reading something else into it."

Way to put your foot in your mouth, Varia. Good thing Lamira is hardly a gossip and won't talk about my slip.

"Whatever..." I grumble. "Are you hungry? I'm starved, and I can't help but notice my cookie stash is missing..."

A sheepish smile stretches across her face, and she holds

her hands out. "In my defense, they're really good cookies."

"*Were* really good cookies. Let's go see if that Jax fellow has any more, or perhaps something just as good."

Lamira links her arm with mine and grins. "Or even better."

There's that irrepressible optimism again. While it helped me get through the dark days of surviving in the hold, it also reminds me of just how undeserving Lamira is of this whole situation. Given her lily-white reputation and lack of lawlessness, it seems to me like the only reason she would have been arrested is if someone in the IHC made the connection between my black-market activities and our friendship. That means that it's all my fault that she's stuck out here in Kilgari space on an alien vessel facing an uncertain future.

I still haven't finished mulling this over when we arrive at the mess hall. Even before we enter the wide portal, the delectable aroma of baked goods reaches us. Lamira and I exchange excited glances.

"Is it me, or does that smell like..." Lamira begins.

And I finish for her. "Chicken pot pie? Hell yes."

Indeed, when I scan the room, I see many of my women enjoying round dishes of what closely resembles the

Terran dish. The meat is dark, so I don't think it's chicken, but my belly is so empty I don't much care.

We rush to the counter as Jax hands out a serving to one of his crewmen. His face stretches in a warm smile as he sees us. I'm glad he's one of the nice chefs instead of one of the high-strung ones who screams at people.

"Welcome back to my humble establishment, Varia." He hands us each a dish with a steaming pie, and my mouth positively waters. "In honor of our human guests, I've made a variation on your classic cuisine, chicken pot pie a la Jax."

"Wow. So, you had chicken to put in these?" Lamira's eyes light up as she takes her pie from Jax's golden-skinned hand.

The head cook looks quite uncomfortable, the gold hue of his cheeks deepening, and he can't meet her gaze when he replies. "Ah...think smaller and more legs."

Lamira's mouth drops open, and I quickly drag her away before she can insult the chef. "C'mon, Lamira, I'm sure it tastes fine. Everyone else seems to be enjoying it."

It's true. I don't see one unhappy person in the mess hall—human or Kilgari. The other day when I was here the two groups seemed to keep to themselves. Now, however, nearly every table holds a mix of Kilgari men and human women.

Lamira and I sit at a small table near the corner with only two seats. After some encouragement from me, she finally stabs her fork into the steaming pie and takes a fully laden bite.

Her eyes widen as she chews, and she can't drive the fork back into her mouth fast enough after she swallows.

"I guess it suits your palate after all?"

She shakes her head. "It's terrible. In fact, it's so bad I can't bear to watch you suffer, so I'll eat your portion and take one for the team."

I brandish my fork and glower menacingly. "You already ate my cookies. Keep your damn hands off my pie or else."

We enjoy a good laugh and for a moment it's like old times, just me and Lamira hanging out and shooting the breeze like we used to do during our time locked in the *Frontier's* hold, when we had literally nothing to do but sit and be held prisoner. The problems sort of fade into the background, but being the person I am I can't keep them off my mind forever.

I wipe my mouth and push in my chair, turning to head for the incinerator. "Duty calls, Lamira."

"Can't you stop working for ten minutes?"

"We've been sitting here for over an hour and there's just too much to be done. Solair was… kind enough to give us a space for exercise, but it needs to be cleared and cleaned and it's too much for one person. Then there's the bedding and other supplies from the *Frontier* to distribute, and…"

"Okay, I get the point." She sighs. "Work crews?"

"Work crews. Help me organize?"

Lamira nods, and we set about disturbing the other diners one by one. For the most part, everyone is not only willing to help, but eager. I think they all like having something to do.

We've got several teams set up between Lamira and me, some to clear the cargo hold and some to assist with fixing up the quarters, when Solair strides into the mess hall.

His gaze meets mine for a moment and then he clears his throat. "Ahem. Forgive me for not getting to this sooner, Varia, but I couldn't help overhearing what you have planned. It seems to me like the work would go much faster indeed if you had some more assistance like we discussed."

"That's certainly true, but I didn't want to keep pushing after yesterday, so we've got it covered."

A thin smile crosses his golden-skinned face. It's a bit cool between us still, but it seems like he wants to get along as much as I do. "Of course, you do. You are responsible and a most capable commander. But please allow me to assign some of my crew to assist you as we had initially agreed, if for no other reason than it will make me feel better about keeping my word."

"I—certainly."

Solair quickly organizes his people, asking for volunteers to join the work crews. There are no shortage of them to be had, and I'm a bit taken aback at how well the two sapient races on the *Queen* get along.

I watch the handsome captain as he moves about the room, speaking to nearly every crewman in turn. I really want to talk to him again, calmly, in private to completely clear the air between us.

But because of my background, I tend to lash out when I feel like I'm backed into a corner. All I want is for Lamira and the other women to be safe, but I don't know how to make that happen.

CHAPTER SIXTEEN

SOLAIR

"Do you have a moment?"

It's the sixth time I've been asked today if I have a moment by a member of my crew, but of course as the commander of this vessel I can't say no. I don't even have to ask why he might possibly need a moment from me because every single conversation that has started with those five words has ended up being about the same thing.

"Of course, Vox—what can I assist you with?" I lead the other male over to my station on the bridge.

"Well… it's the women, Captain—" he starts.

"Of course it is. It's always the women these days," I mutter, wiping a hand over the creases in my brow. I'll look like my grandfather in another year's time if this keeps up. I need to find a planet or space station where I can drop them off that will allow them to find passage back to wherever they need or want to go. It can't be just any backwater planet. I don't want to strand them in the frontiers of space. It's not a nice galaxy and I don't want to cause them additional misery.

But I can't keep going on like this.

So far today, I've been told that the women are lamenting the fact that there isn't enough laundry facilities and they're running out of clean clothes. That they're concerned with sharing rooms with more than one other person. That they're not happy about the lack of produce in the mess. That the ship isn't warm enough for some and it's too warm for others. And, that there's no water for showers.

"I'm sorry if you've heard this before—and I'm not complaining because I do understand that these women desperately require our assistance—but do they have to be so difficult? Is there a better way for us to work together? We do have a common goal, after all," Vox says.

"Do you have a specific issue that's plaguing you, Vox, or just a general sense of annoyance with our new shipmates?"

"Oh, I'm not annoyed with the. Please don't think that. I just feel like we're not all on the same page and everything we try to do to help them just irritates them. They're just being impossible, and they seem to resent the extra work of integrating into our crew," Vox shares.

That won't do at all. Although my crew outnumbers the females on board, it doesn't mean they're sitting around idly. Every male on this ship has duties and I've been nothing but accommodating in rerouting their tasks so they can each take turns assisting Varia and her girls. Hearing that they don't seem to be acting particularly grateful boils my blood, but I keep my emotions in check —again.

After all, it's not the first time I've heard this story today.

"Have you tried talking to any of the women? Maybe if you asked them exactly what's bothering them you might be able to rectify the issues yourselves? Make no mistake. I know I'm the captain of this ship and it's my duty to keep the peace, but I do have other pressing things to deal with."

Vox looks immediately rebuked, but shakes his head. "We just don't know how. We honestly think we're doing what they ask us, but every time something seems to backfire and we end up on the receiving end of a very angry female —although their tactics are more passive than aggressive in nature."

At this, I can't help but think of Varia. I'd much prefer a bit of passivity over her aggression any day.

"Can you provide me with some examples? It would make my job much easier if I had something to present to their leader. Maybe together she and I can come up with a plan to fix them." I'm not at all looking forward to another conversation with said leader.

"Well, just this morning one of the women asked if I could assist her in bringing some items from the cargo hold to her new quarters. I was on my way to the mess, but, not wanting to seem unhelpful, I agreed. I accompanied her to the hold and brought everything she asked me to over to her bunk. I left it on the floor for her to sort, but she quickly grew annoyed at me even though I'd just hauled three boxes that I'm sure weighed more than me across three decks to her new accommodations. Completely baffled, I returned to the mess only to discover I'd completely missed breakfast. Turns out, she was pissed because I'd just 'dumped everything on the floor' and hadn't asked if she wanted help putting it away, but she didn't mention that at the time," Vox explains. I can't help but roll my eyes, an action he immediately latches onto. "I don't understand why she didn't ask for more help. Or, barring that, tell me immediately that she was frustrated with me. Do they know Kilgari can't read minds? I mean, has anyone told them that?"

At this I burst out laughing, despite how unbefitting it is of my role. "We've got a lot to learn about these human women, Vox. I have a feeling it's going to be a long, hard road."

"I assure you that we'll all continue to rise to the occasion, but it'd be nice if they'd just act a little more grateful. I know they've been through a lot, but—all due respect intended, of course—we didn't put them in this situation. A little appreciation of our efforts would be nice," Vox grumbles.

"I agree," I tell him. "Is there anything further you wish to share?"

He shakes his head and turns to leave the bridge, but I stop him.

"Can you do me a favor?" I call out to him once more.

"Of course. Whatever you need."

"Can you tell the crew that I've received enough complaints for one day and that I'll be speaking to Miss Dawn as soon as the opportunity presents itself? I understand your frustrations, but I can't keep being interrupted like this."

"Of course. I'll make sure they know you're looking out for us," he says. "Enjoy the rest of your day."

I throw myself back into my chair once Vox has exited the bridge. A low pounding is starting at the base of my skull and spreading down to my back through the tension in my shoulders. It's been less than three days since these women have taken over my ship and already I feel like if I never see another female again, it'll be too soon.

"They're really keeping the males on their toes, huh?" Grantian speaks from his seat beside me.

He's a lucky bastard, having been kept mostly out of the conflicts with the women due to his status as first mate. When I've been dealing with creating extra space or fielding complaints he's been hidden away up here, overseeing command in my absence.

"I wish I knew how to make it easier on them but it almost seems impossible. We all just have to try our best to work together," I speak without even looking at him, not believing my own words.

"How long do you plan on allowing them to stay? I mean, this isn't a permanent arrangement. Right?" There is no missing the trepidation in his voice.

I can't imagine anything more awful than an extra one hundred and seven individuals aboard my ship, women or otherwise. The *Queen* just doesn't have the means to hold that many long term. Being an older vessel, she's already in need of repairs far more often than a newer ship would be, and I'll never give her up—not for anything or anyone. I'll not replace her in order to accommodate over a hundred females who don't give a shit what ship they're on, so long as they're not chained to it.

"They won't be with us much longer, Grantian. You can be sure of that," I tell him, hoping to assuage his fears. I make a mental note to mention the women's impending departure when I speak with Varia about the other issues.

Grantian only grunts in response.

Taking a deep breath, I pick up my communication unit and patch into Varia's frequency. There's no point in prolonging the inevitable. She and I need to put a stop to the quarreling between our two factions quickly. The last thing I need is a mutiny on my hands or worse—a complete desertion.

"Varia, this is Solair. Can you please join me on the bridge? I have an urgent matter to discuss with you," I speak into the device.

Within seconds I hear her sultry, irritating voice come through loud and clear.

"No can do, Cap—I'm on my way to the med bay. Your doc is apparently planning to open the first of the cryopods, so I need to be there to ensure he doesn't fuck anything up. I'll let you know when I'm available. Over and out," she says.

The sudden sound of dead air on my comm device indicates she's turned hers off completely, clearly uninterested and unwilling to hear anything I have to say. Try as I may, I can barely contain the apprehension I have about Nicari reviving women from cryo. We're already at capacity and now he wants to add more to the mix?

"Better buckle up, Captain. Things are about to get even more interesting," Grantian chuckles.

My response, peppered with curse words that would curl the toes of my dead ancestors, only makes him laugh harder.

CHAPTER SEVENTEEN

VARIA

In preparation for some of the cryopods being opened, I'm wanting to find the best technical mind I know. So before getting to the med bay, I make a slight detour. I continue on down the curving corridors until I come across Thrase. She's ensconced herself on one of the observation decks, pecking away at a data pad while a mug of something hot and steamy rests on a fixed table nearby.

I approach her slowly, so as not to startle her, and stand nearby for several seconds waiting for her to notice me.

When that fails, I politely intrude. "Looks like an engrossing read."

Thrase lifts her gaze from the data monitor and pushes her horn-rimmed glasses up further on her nose.

"Quite." She shows me the title—*Temporal Segregation and the Effects upon Physiognomically Heterogenous Populations of Sapient Species.*

"Uh... is there an abridged version?" I scratch the back of my head and wait for her obliging chuckle. "Listen, if you have some time, I could use your assistance."

"I'd be happy to be of service. Besides, this article is shallow and pedantic at times."

She tucks the pad away in a leather satchel she's acquired somewhere. Judging from the IHC logo, it came from the *Frontier.* She then rises to her feet and we turn to leave the observation deck. I take one last, longing look at the sea of stars and the crimson tones of a distant nebula before the door closes. I wish I had more time to just take in the sights.

"You have yet to enlighten me as to what purpose I might bend my specific set of skills, Varia."

"Oh, sorry." We move to the side of the corridor so several Kilgari can hustle past. They nod at us with anxious smiles on their golden-skinned faces. I keep forgetting they're not used to women being egalitarian. "The Kilgari doctor... what was his name?"

"Nic—Nick something. Nicotine, nectar…it's an N name. It's definitely an N name."

I scoff at her, blowing air out my lips and making my bangs dance.

"I thought you were a genius?"

"Ha ha. Your jest is understood, if not appreciated." Despite her chagrin, Thrase manages to smile. "Besides, even the great Albert Einstein had to write down people's names because he couldn't remember them either."

"Right. Well, Doctor N-something is attempting to open the cryostasis pods of our fellow 'guests' on the *Frontier*, and I'd prefer it if someone with more experience treating humans were present."

"I'll be happy to assist, but…" she gestures down the junction of a different corridor. "…isn't that the way to the *Queen's* medical bay?"

"It is, but we're heading past Fiona's quarters to drag her along, too. She's a whiz with gadgets, so maybe she can help us safely crack those pods open."

"A most prudent decision. Very well."

We head down to Fiona's borrowed quarters and bang on the door like savages. Still no door chimes. But when the door slides back, it reveals a chamber that more closely resembles crew quarters than an unused cargo hold. A poster of circuit schematics adheres to one wall, and a magnetic-lighted end table provides illumination. Fiona herself glances up from the mass of electronics and snake-like, tangled wires when we come in.

"What is it, Varia? Can't you see I'm in the middle of something?"

"Aren't you always?" I grin. "Come on, shut-in, there's a whole ship worth exploring."

"Hard pass." She returns her attention to the exploded device on her bed. Thrase steps forward and clears her throat.

"Allow me, Varia," she speaks more loudly to Fiona. "Oh, Fiona? Would you like to come along and criticize every nuance of a male doctor's procedures?"

"Now you're speaking my language." Fiona unfolds herself from the bed and stretches before falling in behind us. "We're going to Nicari's right?"

"Nicari," I snap my fingers. "That was it."

"Told you it was an N name," Thrase murmurs.

The three of us make our way up to the medical bay, where we find the good doctor Nicari ensconced with four cryopods. I know there were many more than four.

"Doctor Nicari?"

He turns his gaze toward us, flipping up a pair of

magnifying goggles as he does so. Like all of the Kilgari, he's golden skinned and gorgeous, but there's a sort of manic energy to him that seems lacking in the rest of the crew.

"Varia—please, you may call me merely Nicari. No need for formalities. Solair has informed me to assist you in any way I can, no matter how major or minor." He turns back to the pod for a moment and takes a reading, finishing the rest of his speech without eye contact. "Or what I might happen to be engaged in at the moment."

I ignore his passive aggressive comment, though Fiona and Thrase exchange "oh no he did not" glances.

"I appreciate that very much." I walk over to where he's fiddling with the cryopod and clear my throat. "Sorry for being so blunt, Nicari, but where are the rest of the cryopods? There were many more than just four."

"Indeed. I see that your species does not neglect basic mathematics in what passes for your educational system. The remaining active cryopods are stored in cargo bay seven."

My mouth falls open, and I sputter before I can manage to speak.

"C-cargo bay seven? Are you kidding me? They're people, not cargo."

Nicari turns his gaze on me again, and he seems utterly

nonplussed. Like we're discussing the BBL scores off of Novaria and not living beings.

"Of course they are. But like everyone else on board, I am doing the best that I can. Cargo bay seven is a short walk from this lab. Protocol must give way toward practicality in situations like this one."

"Right." I sigh, rubbing my hand over my face. The last thing I want is another argument with a Kilgari. "I get that, okay? But just try to remember that these are living beings inside of these pods."

"Of course. I will make every effort to ensure their safety while I awaken them. Now, excuse me."

He turns away from me and punches keys on the cryopod's panel, but Thrase steps forward, hissing through her teeth.

"What are you doing, you brass-colored primate?" She smacks his hand away from the console.

Nicari seems quite taken aback by her demeanor, and his golden eyes widen even as his lips grow thin and tight. When he speaks, his tone is clipped and icy.

"What I am doing is my job, human. Do you wish the occupants of the pods to awaken or not?"

"I do, but I want them to wake up and not have massive autoimmune disorders. You were about to shut off the MolSta system."

My brow furrows in confusion, as does Nicari's. "MolSta system?"

Thrase flashes her gaze over to me, pushing her glasses up with her finger. "Molecular stabilization system. MolSta, for short." She turns her gaze on Nicari, and her face contorts into a grimace. "Shutting it off could have catastrophic effects on this poor woman's body."

Nicari smiles gently, as if he's dealing with a foolish child.

"Ah, but the backup endocrine system will kick in and keep any damage to a bare minimum."

Thrase's eyes go wide behind her glasses. "Back—backup endocrine system? Are you out of your fucking mind? Humans don't have backup endocrine systems, you dolt."

"Oh. They don't?" He turns toward the pod and scratches the base of one of his horns. "That does complicate things somewhat."

Fiona chooses that moment to interject herself, stepping up to the cryopod's keypad and punching them with rapid finger strokes. "Just as I thought. The good doctor here forgot to recalibrate the biorhythm scanner when he started working on getting the pod unlocked."

I look to her and frown. "Is that bad?"

She laughs, but her eyes are icy and hard. "Only if you don't want them to come out of stasis blind and deaf."

Anger rises inside of me, boiling in my belly until hot words creep up the tip of my tongue. "I. Need. You. To. Be. Honest. Nicari." I shake him to punctuate each word. "Have you ever treated a human before?"

"Well..." he straightens his coat a bit and struggles to regain some of his lost dignity. "To be honest, before we found your derelict ship, I'd never even seen a human before."

"God." I bang my head against the cryopod, not caring that it hurts. "This can't be my life right now. This... this is a clusterfuck waiting to happen." I take a deep breath. "I understand."

How in the hell am I supposed to trust this guy to wake up the other passengers when he can't seem to find his asshole in the dark with a flashlight?

CHAPTER EIGHTEEN

SOLAIR

I've squinted at and re-read the same line on my data pad four times before I finally accept that it might be time to retire for the day. With a sudden influx of one hundred and seven new passengers, it seems like my problems, not to mention my headaches, keep multiplying.

I'm no good to anyone if I don't get some rest. My father used to tell me that the primary objective for the ship's captain is to take care of himself first. While this might sound cruel or selfish, in reality it's just practical. I can't be the one making final decisions if my brain is addled from too little sleep. Well, I suppose I can still be the decider, but I won't be doing a very good job.

My quarters are close to the bridge but it's an unspoken

rule on the *Ancestral Queen* that my men don't come up that stairwell unless it's the direst of emergencies. And even then, only after they've exhausted each and every other possible method of contacting me.

A little bit of solace and solitude isn't too much to ask as the captain—at least I don't think so. I slip out of my garments and stretch out upon my down-stuffed mattress, eschewing my blankets for the time being. Normally I like to keep the temperature on the cool side, but the *Frontier* women complained about it being cold, so we've made an adjustment.

It seems like I've been making a lot of adjustments of late, and to be honest it really rankles. But for the next sleep cycle, I can just close my eyes and enjoy a much-deserved respite from all of my aggravations, problems, and concerns.

My busy mind tries to keep me awake but gradually loses ground before the inexorable march of weariness. Just when I'm about to drift off into the comforting darkness of a hopefully dreamless slumber, the door chime sounds.

It takes me a moment to realize what the sound is. No one's dared to use it in so many years, I'd forgotten what it sounded like. But I sigh and rise from my bed, blinking away the vestiges of attempted slumber.

The chime sounds again and when I snap out a response, my voice is thick with sleep. "I'm coming, dammit."

I start to open the door, but then I recall this is no longer an exclusively male ship. Sighing, I turn back and slip on a pair of trousers just in case a woman is standing outside. And not only do I strongly suspect that it is, in fact, a woman standing in the corridor, but I also have a good idea of the female's identity.

My finger hovers over the entry button for a time while I try to decide if I really want to talk to Varia or not. If she's calling on me in my quarters, I doubt it's because of a happy circumstance, but on the other hand there are no alarm klaxons sounding and the ship doesn't appear to be under attack.

Maybe I could just wait her out and hope she leaves? No. Not this stubborn, fiery creature. In fact, I'm surprised she hasn't rung the chime again—

It sounds once more, as if heralded by my thoughts, and I open the door at last.

As soon as it hisses out of her path, Varia just barges right in without looking directly at me. "It's about goddamn time. Do you have any idea of what's happening down in your medical bay…" Her eyes snap over to me and take in my shirtless form. Varia's gaze widens, and she takes a reflexive step back. "—and you're half-naked."

"I was about to retire for the evening." I rub my eyes and gesture toward one of the two magnetically-adhered padded chairs in my quarters. "But please, have a seat and tell me what has you concerned this time."

"This time? That's a passive aggressive way to put it." Is it just me, or does her gaze keep dipping down to my chest? With what seems a concerted effort, she forces herself to look me in the eyes. "Your so-called doctor was about to either murder one of the *Frontier* women or render them blind and deaf when Thrase and I stopped him."

"What—wait a moment, are you referring to Nicari's attempts to awaken your fellow *Frontier* passengers from cryostasis?" I shake my head and rub the wrinkled flesh beneath the base of my horns. "Is that what's causing you this concern?"

Varia rolls her eyes to the ceiling. "What else would I be referring to? Your doctor doesn't know jack or shit about human physiology." She laughs without mirth—a sharp and cynical sound. "He told me that before you found us floating in space, he'd never even seen a human before. Thanks to him, we nearly lost another girl."

I'm so tired. The last thing I want is another fight, even if she's begging me for one. Rubbing my hand over my eyes, I sit down in the seat across from the empty one I offered to her.

"I can appreciate your concerns, Varia. Really, I can. Nicari is something of an eccentric, even for one of his ilk. He really is quite a skilled doctor, however, and I'm sure that with your woman—Thrase, was it?—assisting him, the two of them will figure out how to safely awaken your fellow passengers."

I gesture again at the empty seat. Varia heaves an exasperated sigh and settles herself onto it. I shift a bit because our knees touch slightly, and I don't want to make her uncomfortable.

"It would be nice if they could be in possession of all their faculties when they thawed out, too." She crosses her arms over her chest and fixes me with a stern glare. Even when she's angry she manages to be attractive, and again I feel the swell of certainty in my soul that this is meant to be my mate, all appearances to the contrary aside.

"Please try to have a little faith in both Nicari and Thrase. Will you? This is an unusual situation for us all and we're all just doing the best we can."

Varia uncrosses her arms and sinks wearily into the chair. The anger drains somewhat from her face, and I'm a bit troubled by the dark circles lurking beneath her normally bright eyes.

"I know. I know..." she makes a dismissive gesture with her hand. "I don't mean to come across as such a bitch, you know."

I rest my chin on my palm and nod sagely.

"The pressures of command do weigh rather heavily upon one. Do they not?"

"Command?" She flicks her gaze over to me for a moment before returning it to the floor. "I guess that's an apt term. But unlike you, I never sought out the responsibility. I never wanted to be a leader, not really."

"Perhaps, but there's an old saying in the galaxy." I lean forward and flash her a gentle smile. "Great people do not seek out power, but have it thrust upon them. Perhaps your gods have decided that you and you alone are the best suited for this task."

"I'm not sure I believe in any of the old Terran gods." She sighs and shakes her head while a helpless laugh escapes her lips. "I mean, the other women and I have been through hell, and I just don't see why a loving or kind god might allow that to happen."

When she's not angry, especially not angry at me, I find Varia to be far more complex and compelling than appearances would suggest. Would I be any less stressed and determined if it were my own crew thrust into such a situation? Perhaps I'm just tired, but I speak before I really think about what I'm saying.

"I, for one, am glad your path has led you here."

Varia does look at me now, her eyes wide, questioning. She leans forward, her voice coming in a husky whisper. "Are you? Are you really?"

She's so close to me now that I can smell her sweet scent and feel the heat emanating from her skin. All of a sudden the wall of anger between us has melted away, leaving nothing to obstruct my lips as I move in for a kiss without really considering what's happening.

Varia tilts her face to the side, parts her lips as if to accept my kiss... and then abruptly stands up.

"I—I have to go and..."

I just sit there like a slumbering Odex while she rushes out the door, leaving me very alone and very confused.

CHAPTER NINETEEN

VARIA

What the fuck is wrong with me?

I went to Solair's quarters, despite Nicari being aghast at the very idea, so I could take him to task for the incompetence of his underlings. In what universe does that scenario end with me on the verge of kissing him? That scenario end with me on the verge of kissing him?

Shit. One minute I want to throttle the living daylights out of the Kilgari captain, and the next I want him to climb on top of me. God, I wish he wasn't so damn good looking. Maybe if he hadn't greeted me at the door with those chiseled pecs and sleek abs on display. His tapered torso just seems to invite my gaze to keep going down further, to the prominent bulge in his trousers that has (allegedly) two members. As if I don't have enough going on in my head at the moment.

I return to my quarters and quietly slip into bed so as not to disturb my bunkmates. Lamira is snoring softly in hers, but I notice Thrase is nowhere to be seen. Hopefully she's keeping a watchful eye on Doctor Quack so he doesn't randomly kill one of the poor women still in cryostasis.

Lying there in the dark, the hum of the ship's engines is a soothing sound, yet I find I can't be lulled into sleep. My mind is too jumbled, too filled with conflicting emotions and ideas. I'm not used to feeling like this, and I don't like it one bit.

Ask anyone and they'll tell you Varia Dawn is nothing if not sure of herself. Don't get me wrong. I'm not naïve. I don't think for a moment that I know everything or have all the answers. For example, I'd never try to second guess Fiona on how an electrical panel should be wired. But once I decide on a course of action, I don't spend a lot of time second guessing my choice.

But here I am, second guessing everything I feel about the handsome Kilgari captain. Part of me wonders if we'd be at each other's throats so much if the circumstances of our first meeting had been different. There's no way to know for sure but thinking about it certainly tangles my mind and prevents even the idea of sleep.

Eventually, I give up on the idea of slumber for the time

being and fling my covers back. I dress in loose fitting trousers and a tank top before heading out into the darkened corridor. My feet take me toward the cargo bay Solair gifted me as a workout space.

When the doors slide open, I'm surprised by what I see. For one thing, the bay has been cleared and cleaned with a meticulous eye for detail. I don't know where all of the fishing equipment—the heavy, awkward, pain in the ass fishing equipment—wandered off to, but I don't care. I only know that it's been replaced with rubber mats, magnetically locking barbells—don't want those flying around during an emergency—and what appears to be a drinking fountain recently installed right into the wall.

The other thing that surprises me is that I'm not alone. Apparently, I've interrupted the end of a work bullshit session that seems to spring up in any sapient race engaged in manual labor. A group of Kilgari men stand about in casual poses, though their gazes snapped over to me when the door opened.

A moment later, their matriarchal conditioning kicks in and they politely look away and return, albeit a bit stiffly, to their previous conversations. I move into the bay-turned-workout room and slip off my shoes before stepping barefoot onto the practice mat.

I take some time to stretch, putting my hands behind my head and leaning backward before working on my hamstrings. It's been a while since I was able to really get a good workout in. Who knows how long I was in cryo? All I know is that my muscles complain with the stiffness of inactivity and then gradually loosen into limp submission as I continue my stretch routine.

Once I'm sufficiently warmed up, I start practicing a few strikes. I've definitely slowed down some since I went into the cryopod, but I feel like I can get back to where I was in relatively short order.

Over time I realize I've gained something of an audience. The Kilgari crewmen are watching my movements intently. Not in a creepy way, like they're trying to check out my body, but in an appreciative manner. Finally, one of them overcomes generations of conditioning and steps toward the mat. "You're really good. Is that Khur Lei?"

"What?" I burst into laughter. "I'm pretty sure that's a fake style made up by the holovid entertainment industry. I practice several styles, but most of my training is in Magate."

"Magate?" he tilts his head to the side in query. I notice this Kilgari isn't quite as powerfully built as the rest, but he has an easy smile and a very nonthreatening manner that makes me willing to relax around him. "I've never heard of it."

"It's a Terran art developed shortly after we started exploring the galaxy. About a third of the moves are designed for zero g combat, but the strikes are universal."

"That's fascinating. I used to study Raith Pa style, but then I found out my supposed teacher had never even been in one of their monasteries." He licks his lips nervously before speaking again. "Ah... would you be willing to teach me a little?"

I start to say no, but then I realize that having a sparring partner isn't a bad idea at all. "Sure, I'll show you some things... sorry, I haven't caught your name."

"Vurt. Pleased to meet you."

"Call me Varia. Like your captain, I've no patience for formalities."

"Very well. Varia." He grins. "Both of our names begin with an unvoiced labiodental fricative. Isn't that neat?"

"Ah, sure."

Vurt isn't the most agile male I've ever seen, but he's a good listener and replicates the basic stances with aplomb. I find that by instructing him I remember things about Magate I'd forgotten, and even learn new ways to polish up my own technique.

We're in the middle of a sticky hands drill, where the defender tries to break the attacker's grip but is constantly foiled by perpetual motion, when I decide to pry a little into Vurt's head.

"Say, Vurt... how long have you served with Solair?

He blinks sweat out of his eyes as our limbs slap together with meaty thunks. "Oh, more than a year, I guess. Why?"

"I was just wondering… what kind of male is he?"

Vurt pauses, and I let up on the drill so we can both catch our breath. "Well, ah… he's a Kilgari."

Struggling to keep the frustration out of my tone, I rephrase my query. "No, I mean… what's his character like? Is he a good commander? Does his crew like him, as well as respect his authority?"

"Oh." Vurt shakes his head. "Well, I don't interact with him as much as some of the bridge crew, but he's always struck me as a decent sort. He's tough, but fair, and not a disciplinarian like some commanders."

"A disciplinarian?"

"Yeah, I mean he doesn't assign shit details to people he's mad at. Hell, I don't even think I've ever heard him yell outside of an emergency situation. That's not how he acts when you fuck up."

I purse my lips, absorbing this new information. "I see. So, what does he do when someone, as you so subtly put it, fucks up?"

Vurt grins in response. "Oh, he doesn't have to yell. He gets this look on his face." Vurt assumes a comically accurate expression similar to the dour disappointment I've often seen on Solair's golden-skinned face, so much so that I burst into laughter. "Vurt..." I laugh even harder because he's really nailed Solair's deep baritone. "I'm very disappointed in you."

"That's really good. Do you ever do that impression in front of him?"

"Are you out of your mind? Of course not." Our laughter dies down, and he grins. "We Kilgari tend toward politeness and a reserved composure."

"So I've noticed. What's your world like?"

Vurt sighs and rubs his chin thoughtfully. "Well, we're one of the first members of the League... but you're probably asking about what our society is like. Right? Basically, we used to be more male dominated as a culture until our dumb asses killed off most of the females in a civil war."

I gape in astonishment. "That's awful."

"Indeed, and it nearly meant the end of us as a species. But since females were so scarce, they sort of took advantage of their new importance. They taught us that conflict should be used as a last resort, or not at all. Honestly, if I'm lucky enough to be a fourth or fifth husband, I look forward to what I'll learn from my future, hypothetical wife."

"Fifth husband? Is the divorce rate really that high on Kilgar?"

"Divorce rate?" He shakes his horned head. I notice the

other observing Kilgari seem just as confused. "What's a divorce rate?"

"I'll take that as a no..." I put two and two together in my head and gasp. "Wait a minute. You mean that your females are polyandrous?"

Realization dawns in his eyes. "Yes, that's it. Each female might have up to a dozen husbands. It's the only way to repopulate our world, as monogamous relationships are no longer practical."

Gradually the sparring session breaks down into a crash course on Kilgari society and history. I'm a little bit shocked by what I hear, but overall, they seem a people of good moral stock.

It's all fascinating, but I'm still no closer to understanding my feelings for Solair before I head back to my bunk.

CHAPTER TWENTY

Solair

Despite the two nagging distractions quaking just south of my navel, I did manage to slip off into sleep. After all of the excitement and upset our new charges have kicked up, my night was blessedly dreamless, so I suppose wishes do come true.

When the gentle sounds from my data pad pull me back to consciousness, the first thing that floods into my brain is the image of Varia in the moment before she bolted. Those half-lidded eyes and gently parted lips. The moment had been so fleeting, but I'm kicking myself for not making the most of the opportunity when it came. At least I would have an answer as to whether or not she's my true mate.

RESCUED BY THE ALIEN PIRATE

"Dammit, Solair," I grunt to myself as I sit up.

I must have been deeply asleep, as groggy as I am. My trousers are still on the floor where I kicked them off, so I yank them on before meandering over to splash some water—a benefit of being Captain—on my face. The next move is to get myself fueled up for the day ahead.

Walking to the bridge, I can't help but rankle slightly at the gall of that woman, presuming upon my private time. She's got some backbone. I can say that for her. I find myself wondering why none of my men were on hand to forestall her approach. It's a pretty distracted world aboard right now.

"What the hell?"

I can hear the startling din before I can even get close to the dining hall. My jaw drops at the sheer volume of it, and I consider turning back before I even reach the door. Surely, I could find someone who could just bring a plate up to the relative serenity of my own quarters?

But maybe Varia will be in there. The prospect of seeing her gives me the steel I need to stride into the cacophony awaiting me.

It's madness in here. If Varia is in this hurricane, I'd be hard pressed to pick her out. It's so loud it almost makes it hard to focus. The room is filled with women. Why does everyone have to speak so loudly?

"I've never had food like this before!"

"Yeah, well, I hope I never have anything like it again."

"I like it."

"How long do you think we're going to be stuck on this ship?"

"I wouldn't call it 'stuck' exactly!"

"I'm in no hurry to get away from all this. Are you?"

It's like they're all talking at once and nobody is listening. Responses that do line up seem incidental at best. Like some kind of happy accident.

There's this phenomenon where one group's conversation becomes so loud that other groups have to speak up even to hear themselves. So the first group tops them, and it grows until the whole world is thrown into utter pandemonium. But this is something else.

Human women seem to inspire some kind of hysteria in each other. The room is thick with high-pitched voices and shocking bleats of piercing laughter. Even if this isn't the new standard, it makes me wonder what the hell I am going to do with all these women. The mind reels.

I've been in the heated pitch of battle before, but this is wholly overwhelming. Once, so long ago I can hardly remember the circumstances, I found myself in a Targelian bat coop. That brand of squawking and flapping and general anarchy is the closest thing I can compare this to. I'm sorry if that doesn't sound like a compliment, but it's not supposed to.

"So, wait, how do you pronounce where you're from again?"

That was a man's voice.

My eyes seem to focus for the first time, and I find members of my crew peppered throughout the mayhem. If I'm affronted by all of this, I seem to be the only one. The faces of the men I can see are lighted with broad, bright smiles.

"Am I really the first nonhuman you've ever seen? Where have you been hiding yourself?"

"Don't pester her, Trimlan. She's the first human you've ever seen. I'd call that even."

"If you can tell which one of these creatures you saw first, I'll buy every drink you have for a month."

"I can remember exactly which one!"

Shrieks of laughter bubble up and the throaty braying of my own men matches it. What looks like mindless conversation begins to take on a kind of pattern. Order emerges from the chaos, and the truth of the situation hits me like a bolt from the far edge of the cosmos.

This is part of the human mating ritual.

At least it seems to be. The room is flooded with various aromas, and while the particular strain I recognize as my own mate isn't in the mix, I've no doubt that others are catching the scent. It would certainly speak to why none of my men have been readily found at their workstations since our visitors joined us.

This unexpected hitch in the journey might just be a fortuitous event.

"Are you really expecting us to stay in some cargo hold? All of us?"

"I wish it weren't the case, miss, but those seem to be the orders from above."

"But it's so much livelier up here with all of you."

"I can agree with that, miss. Absolutely."

Breaking past the grand swirl of the room I begin to see the tiny interactions, touches, and looks. It seems like everything is an invitation. And the men are reveling in it.

One of the primary reasons I departed Kilgar was to escape the rigors of being kept in a harem. It's no secret that our men are prized for their prowess between the sheets. Shit, it's a point of pride. But even the greatest pleasure becomes a drudgery when there's no choice. But now choice seems to abound at every turn. These women damn near equal us, number for number. While it would be absurd to think that most of my crew would find their true match by such a fluke of circumstance, it does take a bit of the sting off of my own, taunting predicament.

It's one thing to be tied as a group to an elite number of powerful females who can use us at and for their pleasure. But to be able to choose—really choose? It's almost too much to hope.

"Have you ever seen anything like this?"

Swipt has materialized at my side in that unnerving way he has. I just shake my head and survey the scene.

"How long have you been here?" I ask.

"Long enough to watch you start to put the pieces together. Who could have expected a little rescue mission to turn into something like this?" He leans in closer, "Have you, uh, detected anything... specific?"

I look at him, uncomprehending until he taps the side of his nose. The boldness of his question breaks in upon me and I can feel the blood racing to my face.

"Hard to say. You?"

"Hard to say," he echoes me, giving a loose shrug and turning back to watch the show. "We should call Nicari up here."

"Why is that?"

"I'd say this is a pretty interesting case study. Wouldn't you? Even if there aren't a lot of..." he taps his nose again.

"You can't argue with the fact that this whole ship is about to turn into a pleasure cruise."

I snort at the thought.

"Just so long as everyone keeps at their post. At least part of the time."

"What do you think the chances of that are?" He's cut a sideways smile to me before curling through the door and ambling down the hall.

Trying to use a scientist's eyes, I look back at the throng of people cackling at each other. Maybe he's right. Maybe I should get Nicari up here. He could fill the dictation files of a data pad inside of twenty minutes trying to break down the behavioral displays unfolding on every side.

There's every chance that most of the crew runs the risk of finding a mate among this mass of women. It's a massive thing to consider, but everything I've seen since bringing these women on board seems to bear it out. In a funny way, it also makes me feel less alone with the storm raging inside my own chest.

CHAPTER TWENTY-ONE

Varia

I stare at the top of my bunk and sigh.

Even though it's already morning—or breakfast time, since there really isn't any sunrise aboard the *Ancestral Queen*—it's a struggle to get out of bed. Exhaustion pulls at me, my constant dreams of a slow death in a dark cargo hold stopping me from having a proper night of sleep. Still, I kick the blankets away and swing my legs off the bed. It's no use lying here and think of yesterday. Yawning loudly, I stretch my back and force myself out of the room.

By now, the ship's corridors are already abuzz with activity. Kilgari crewmen amble from one corridor to another, performing the *Ancestral Queen's* daily circuitry maintenance, and I immediately spot Fiona and Ilya among them. While one is busy debating the merits of replacing some of the circuitry, the other's busy dismantling a cooling system panel under the surprised gaze of a Kilgari mechanic.

I still can't wrap my head around how quickly the rest of the women adjusted to life here. They should be worrying about their future, as we'll all have tough decisions to make, but most of them don't seem particularly concerned with any of that. They seem happy to be here, and they seem even happier to have the Kilgari as their crew mates. It's insane.

We're not staying here.

I can't stay here. I have a responsibility to make sure these women get home.

All my life I've been told that the galaxy is a dangerous and yet wonderful place. That humanity is just one of a myriad of species in the galaxy, but that the benevolence of the Interstellar Human Confederation will protect us in our homes and through our travels.

Well, if the IHC really did arrest me and all these women, that belief was nothing more than bullshit.

Our government is supposed to protect us from the bad guys. The Kraaj. The Ataxian Coalition. The Reapers.

But we aren't supposed to fear our own government.

We need to get back. To set the world as we know it right again.

Shaking my head, I make my way toward the dining hall. It's not hard. All I have to do is follow the noise made from dozens of women chattering nonstop, all of it punctuated with the occasional deep Kilgari laugh. I stand in the doorway, trying to look for a vacant seat, when I notice Solair sitting at one of the corner tables with Swipt.

I rock on my heels for a couple of seconds, not sure if I should approach him. I was harsh with him, especially when considering he could just shove us all out the airlock, and now I feel guilty. Gritting my teeth, I rake one hand over my face and make my peace with what I have to do. I might not know when to shut up, but I do know when it's time for an apology.

"All right, let's do this," I mutter under my breath, cutting through the rows of long tables as I make my way toward the corner. Swipt is the first to notice me. He falls silent mid-sentence, clears his throat, and quickly melts away from the table. "I think we need to talk, Solair."

"You didn't come here to argue. Did you?" Turning around on his seat so that he's facing me, Solair sighs. "At least eat something."

"No, I didn't come here to argue," I reply, but I have to

make an effort not to snap at him. Why did he assume I came here to argue? It's not like I'm some insufferable bitch who's always complaining. Right?

Right?

Taking the seat across from him, I clear my throat and straighten my back. "In fact, I came here to apologize."

"Is that so?" He cocks up one eyebrow and leans back. "Huh."

"Don't 'huh' me." With a frown, I force myself to continue. "I know you're doing your best to help us out, and that you owe us nothing. I'm sorry for my outburst. It's just that..." I trail off and stare down at my hands as I try to think of my next words. "I'm scared for them. You know? They're innocent—for the most part—and I want to make sure they'll be safe. They deserve to be safe. The galaxy is not a nice place, but these women grew up knowing their leaders would take care of them. And we need to get them back to their lives so that promise isn't broken."

"I understand that." Smiling, he gives me one slight nod. When my eyes meet his, he rises to his feet and waves toward the exit. "Care to join me for a walk? It's impossible to have a conversation in here."

"Agreed," I laugh. With almost a hundred people stuffed inside the dining room, the background noise is akin to that of an angry swarm of wasps. We walk out of the room side by side and, from the far corner of the room, Lamira spots me and gives me a little wave. More than just a wave, she also gives me a conspiratorial wink. I wave back at her discreetly, ignoring her wink, and march after Solair.

"It's been awhile since I've had this many people aboard the *Queen*," Solair speaks as we amble down a long corridor, one leading into the ship's stern. There's not a soul around us, and the contrast is striking. It's so peaceful here that I can almost hear the faint flicker of the lights mounted overhead. "In fact, I don't think I've ever had this many people aboard."

"We're a nuisance. I get it."

"That's not what I meant." He frowns. "The logistics are tough, sure, but my crew don't seem to mind the women. Besides, all of you are trying to help us. It's not like you're freeloaders. That's because of you, I think—as their captain, you're doing a good job."

"I'm not their captain," I whisper, and Solair stops walking and turns to face me.

"But you are," he insists. "You're the one they look up to."

"I don't know about that."

"Look out there." Taking one step toward me, he lays one hand on my shoulder and turns me around. He points toward the large glass panel on the wall, one offering an expansive view of space, and for a moment neither of us say a thing. We just look at the million stars outside, strewn across the dark canvas of space like grains of sand on a beach. "Some people look outside and see the romance that comes with being among the stars. People like us, Varia, we see the dangers in it. Not because we don't appreciate the beauty, but because we feel responsible for those enchanted by it. You worry about them, and you care about them… if that doesn't make you their captain, I don't know what does."

"Is that how it is with you?" I do my best not to focus on the way his fingers remain on my shoulder. Something about his touch makes it hard to think, almost as if his hand is electrified and is zapping my thoughts before they have a chance to form.

"You bet it is," he replies, a kind smile spreading across his lips. "Some of my warriors are perfectly happy living day to day. They don't care about much, and they're content doing whatever I tell them to do. As for me… well, there's a lot I worry about, and it never stops."

"Yeah, I know that feeling." Returning his smile, I look into his eyes and my heart tightens. When I first saw him, bursting into the transport ship like some warrior out of a storybook, I never thought he'd be this… kind. Back then, he emanated that sexiness that came with being a dangerous savage, but it seems like there are layers to him.

"Thank you for everything you're doing. I might not always show it, but I really am thankful."

"No need to thank me," he says, his voice dipping into a whisper. "And just so you know, there's no need for you to leave. It might not be easy, but I won't kick you out." Allowing his smile to transform into a grin, he gives my shoulder a soft squeeze. "As annoying as you might be, I actually enjoy having you around."

"I know," I breathe out, and my heart tightens even more as I imagine myself spending more time with him. It wouldn't even have to be aboard the *Queen*. Anywhere would be fine, just as long as I didn't have to leave his side.

Get a grip, my inner voice suddenly chimes in, batting away all those lewd thoughts. It's useless. As long as my eyes remain on Solair's, there's no controlling what happens inside my mind. Something about him draws me in. His presence is magnetic, his gaze is irresistible, and—

Get a hold of yourself, Varia, my inner voice returns, but this time I don't pay it any attention. I just push it into a dark corner of my mind and let my instincts take the steering wheel. It's not hard to do—in fact, it feels like the right thing to do.

Never looking away from me, Solair takes his hand from my shoulder and raises it. Slowly, almost as if I was a deer that might get startled, he lays his fingers on my face. The moment I feel his touch on my skin, my eyelids flutter and my heart kicks and punches against my ribcage.

When he leans into me, I offer no resistance.

I want it.

I need it.

CHAPTER TWENTY-TWO

SOLAIR

I feel the spark of the mating bond the moment my lips touch hers. It's as if thousands of eons of time come together to form this single moment. She and I are the only ones alive in this galaxy, in this entire universe, brought together by fate or some unknown gods. I let myself sink into the sensations, the bond infusing into every cell, neurons and synapses firing. My heartbeat quickens as my blood thrums through my veins to the pulse of an echoing whisper: *mate, mate, mate.*

Kissing Varia is like hearing a song I used to know but hadn't heard in a very long time. Even though I've never kissed her before, it feels like a memory. Like it happened in a dream or sometime long ago. My soul knows how to kiss her, effortlessly.

We're standing in the aft of the *Queen*. Outside, the stars splay out before us in a perfect spill against the pitch-black sky, visible through the massive window. They twinkle and burn fiercely, as if just for us. I couldn't have planned a more romantic setting if I'd tried.

As my lips move against hers, I remember a passage from the Elder Scrolls of the Kilgar. It states, simply, "through lips entwined a mate is found, forever and ever the two shall be bound." I don't know how my people have come so far from that concept, especially not now that I'm experiencing it firsthand. I know we were nearly decimated and had to adjust our way of life to ensure the perpetuation of our race, but to completely turn our backs on the idea of fated mates seems ludicrous. This feels so completely right that I can't imagine going back to living any other way.

The Precursors, in all their teachings, were right.

When one finds his mate, the feeling is like nothing he has, or will, experience.

I'm quickly brought out of my thoughts and back to the present when Varia's tongue glides across the seam of my lips. If she seeks to deepen the kiss, who am I to deny her? I open my mouth and instantly feel the smooth velvet of her tongue slide against mine, sensuously, as if the taste of me is a drug to her and she needs her fix.

Truly, her actions are those of a woman starved for affection. She presses her lithe body against mine, from her breasts down to her feet, wrapping her arms around my neck and a leg around my ankle to pull me in closer to her. I waste no time lifting her into my arms, holding her tightly against me as I walk her back toward the ledge of the window. Once seated, she twists both legs around my waist, locking me against her in a coiled embrace.

Her hands grasp the taut skin of my back, the nails of her fingers digging tiny crescents into my flesh as she clings to me. The sharpness of them brings a sense of pleasure along with the pain. I lift my hands to tangle in the wildness of her hair, holding her mouth on mine as I fight the urge to completely devour her. She's so damn hot I can barely stand it.

I should have known this would happen. After all, I've suspected she's my mate since the moment I first laid eyes on her. That, combined with the fact that we can barely stop arguing, should have made it clear that all the tension between us would eventually catch fire. We've been tiptoeing around an explosion for days.

I don't know how much humans know about the Kilgari way of life, but I'm sure she doesn't know about the mating bond. Not many do, especially now that we've moved to a polyamorous lifestyle. I wonder if she felt a pull toward me too, and if this is all just the culmination of that, or if she's also wanted me all this time. Either way, kissing her like this is more than I could have ever dared to hope for, and I don't want to stop.

I'm nearly drowning in the idea that she could be mine. Humans aren't usually the polyamorous type. When they take a partner, they typically do so in pairs of two. The thought of never having to share her with another male is foreign, yet wondrous. It thrills me to know she will be mine alone.

Her hands move from my back to rest on the sides of my face, fingers tentative as they drift up to touch my horns. From how gentle they suddenly become, I wonder if she's never touched a pair before. She strokes them softly, sending a shock of desire straight to my belly. Clearly, she has no idea how sensitive they are—or maybe she does, and this is just another attempt to drive me completely mad with lust.

Whatever her intentions, it works. With a low growl, I pull her even closer to me. I feel her heavy, ample breasts flatten against my chest, her nipples tight peaks against the thinness of her shirt. A moan escapes her throat as they rub against the hardness of my chest. I can't stop myself from pushing a hand between us to claim one between my fingers. She jumps in surprise and pulls her mouth away from me for only a moment, just so she can catch my gaze. She gives me a knowing smile before crashing her lips back down onto mine.

My gods. This woman—this amazing creature—will surely be the death of me.

Delicious warmth floods down to my groin, pooling into both of my members. I know she can feel them straining through the thick fabric of my pants—not a difficult feat when there are two of them and they're proportioned to my massive body. I've never been with a human before, but I'm sure her physiology is similar to other females I've coupled with. I angle my hips closer to hers and brush both cocks against her mound, delighting in the gasp it elicits from her.

What I don't delight in, however, is how she immediately pulls away after that gasp. As if the feel of our desirous parts grazing against each other brings her back to her senses, quickly and crashing. She completely detaches herself from me and drops down off the ledge, placing a fair distance between us.

The absence of her lips against mine is acute and tortuous. I want them back.

"What's the matter?" I'm dumbfounded over how quickly she could stop.

"I'm sorry, I just—anyone could find us here," she states, as if I didn't know that already.

I just don't care. Let anyone stumble upon us. It doesn't matter. The only thing that matters is that we're here, together, finally.

"I assure you, not many venture here. Did I do something wrong? Did I hurt you?"

It's entirely possible. Sometimes I don't know my own strength and maybe the reproductive organs of human females are exceedingly sensitive.

"No—no, you didn't hurt me. It's just—I still have so much work to do and you and I... I don't want to further complicate things between us. We need to be able to work together to solve this mess we're in and I don't want anything to get in the way of that. I don't want a casual tryst between us to jeopardize the wellbeing of anyone on this ship." Her voice trails off, as if she's desperately trying to convince herself that we shouldn't be together.

It's completely foolish for her to do so. She may give as good as she gets and push every single one of my buttons, but nothing in the 'verse could tear us apart if she agreed to be mine—not even her.

"Varia, I truly don't think you have anything to worry about—" I start, but she cuts me off.

"Please, Solair. Let's just forget this ever happened, okay? Chalk it up to a bad move on my part. I apologize." Her big, doe eyes are pleading.

Even before I confirmed she is my mate, I'd never do anything to upset her, so I nod and back away to give her space. Without another word she departs, leaving me alone with my thoughts.

I return to the window and stare out at the galaxy, eyes focused on the stars. It's amazing to think some of them have already burnt themselves out, yet are so far away the light is only reaching us now. I wonder how many scenes like this the stars have borne witness to. How many lovers have embraced beneath them, heedless of their eternal gaze?

I wish I weren't, but I'm frustrated with Varia's hasty departure. I wish she would have stayed and talked to me; trusted me enough to share why she's so scared to let me in. I know there's a reason for it. I just can't figure out what it is.

She's my mate, but maybe I should just let her go. There's no hope for us if she can't find it within herself to not run from me every time I try to get close to her. I can't continue baring my soul to her if she's not interested in all I have—and want—to offer her.

Maybe I should just drop her and all the rest of the women off at the nearest IHC space port and be done with it. Being without her would be difficult, but not as difficult as it would be if she were to remain here and not be mine.

As I make my way back to the bridge, I can't even fathom the thought.

CHAPTER TWENTY-THREE

VARIA

Fingers brushing my lips, I rush away from the handsome Kilgari captain's presence. This is crazy. I'm no prude, but I'm not one to just swap spit with a man who has so much power over me.

This is a path I'm not sure I should follow. There had been nothing short of pure electricity the first time his lips brushed my own. It was as if my heart, long dormant, had begun to pump blood through my cold, dead system again. Yes, I shut him down, but I really didn't want to. My main concern was someone seeing us together, which is another conundrum I must unravel.

As I wander through the burnished, baroque corridors of the *Ancestral Queen*, the engine's comforting throb is not the only sound that greets my ears. Laughter, both male and female, seems to emanate from everywhere. Well, it seems like most of the *Frontier* women are certainly getting along with our alien hosts, and vice versa.

The chemistry had been perfect with Solair, no question of that. So why did I flee at the first opportunity? I could have just waited until he inevitably invited me back to his private cabin. A little thrill shoots through me that I've already been there, up the forbidden staircase that his men fear to tread upon.

I can't sort all of this out on my own. My first thoughts are of Lamira. While she might be less worldly than the rest of the *Frontier* women—particularly those who have a somewhat shady past, as I do—she possesses something I can only call "hearth wisdom." Lamira isn't the type of person who agonizes over the right thing to do. She just knows it innately in her heart.

That's one of the reasons I think I've been drawn to her throughout our friendship. Her easy nature is a contrast to my own anxious, somewhat high-strung personality. Between the two of us, we balance each other out.

I find her in our makeshift quarters, and at first I believe she's entertaining company because there are many voices echoing into the corridor. But when the door slides open, my mouth falls open in shock because she has a working holovid projector.

"You've been holding out on me!" I come over and sit cross-legged on her bed so I'm in the right position to take in the gorgeous colors and textures of the emitter. It's one of the good ones, a Durzacorp model.

"I have not." She punches me softly in the bicep. "First Mate Grantian gifted it to me. He heard me complaining about missing *As the Galaxy Churns* and wanted to help."

I settle in next to her and squint at the display of two Alzhon actors in "Terran face" cosmetics trying to reenact a poor rip-off of Romeo and Juliet. How Lamira can watch this schlock and not want to hang herself from the ceiling is beyond me, but to each their own.

"Well, can you stop streaming the broadcast for a moment? I was hoping to talk to you about something."

"Sure." Lamira's face creases with a worried frown before she addresses the holo projector. "Cease playback, *As the Galaxy Churns* season sixteen."

Then she turns her gaze on me, eyes narrowing as she attempts to ascertain what's eating me.

"Hmmm." Her face stretches in a slight grin. "Well, it's not an emergency, or you wouldn't be talking to me. You'd be yelling at the good-looking Kilgari captain to fix it."

I hide my face in my hands when she brings up Solair. At first Lamira thinks my reaction means she's gone too far, and she puts her hand on my shoulder.

"Hey, I'm sorry, I didn't mean that you yell. Well, not all the time..."

"It's not that." My voice is muffled by my hands, but I keep my face covered to hide my shame. "It is about Solair, though."

"Oh no. Did he ask us to leave?"

I shake my head, groaning behind my hands.

"No? Then, I don't understand. Did you guys have another fight?"

Again, I shake my head. I hear a sudden intake of air through clenched teeth, and then I feel Lamira's hands pulling on my wrists, forcing me to look at her.

"Did you hurt him?"

I roll my eyes to the ceiling and swiftly stand up, hugging my arms across my torso as I wander toward the far wall. "No, I didn't hurt him, Lamira. Fuck, am I such a terrible, rage-filled beast that everyone assumes the worst about me?"

"Come on, Var, I didn't mean it like that." She comes over to me and hugs me from behind. "If you're hurting, I'm hurting. Let me help you. Tell me what's going on."

She takes my hand and tugs me back toward the bed as some boring news broadcast goes on in the background.

Lamira laughs and pats my hand. "It can't be that bad."

"Or maybe it can." I have to squeeze my eyes shut as I make my confession. "I... just left Solair, and we'd been, um... kissing."

Lamira's eyes go wide, her mouth forms an O, and for a moment I think she's going to start berating me for being impulsive. But then she lets out a childish whoop and pumps her fist in the air. "Yes, girl! Get up on that golden-skinned beast!"

Now it's my turn to gape in astonishment. "Lamira! Behave yourself. This is serious!"

"I *am* being serious." She gently shakes my shoulders in comic rage. "There's nothing wrong with seeing something you want and going for it."

"Lamira, I love you like a sister, but you're not thinking things through. I don't even know how long we're going to be on this ship, let alone Kilgari space. Where could this... this thing between us possibly lead?"

Lamira purses her lips and folds her legs under her, adopting a more somber expression. "That's one way to look at it... or, you could just see it as an opportunity to have some fun while we're on board..."

"Lamira!" She's full of surprises tonight. "I can't believe what's coming out of your mouth. And here I thought you were so innocent."

"Innocent?" She laughs. "Maybe compared to some of the

convicts on the *Frontier*, but that doesn't mean I never think about sex."

"Oh god. Please stop." I clap my hands over my ears. "I don't know when or if we'll be headed back to IHC space, and anyway, I thought he despised me until the other day in his quarters."

"You've been in his quarters?"

"Shut up. Yes, we stopped arguing for a bit and just sort of talked. I almost let him kiss me that night, but then today... it just kind of happened."

"Hmm." Lamira puts a finger to her lips and her gaze grows distant. "So, you think maybe he actually feels the same attraction you do?"

I sigh and pick at the fibers on the bedspread. "I know he does. He—during our spirited make-out session, he said something like 'you could be mine.'"

Lamira's hand flies in front of her mouth, and she gets as giddy as a schoolgirl.

"Oh my god, that's fantastic. That's just the kind of thing you want a big, hunky golden alien to say, especially one with two..."

I hold up my hand to forestall further comments. "Can we not bring that up again, please? This is confusing enough without... without having to bring *that* into the mix."

"My lips are sealed." Lamira throws her hands up in the air, and then she settles back ostensibly to finish watching her show. "But you know you've thought about it at least a few times."

"I've thought about smothering you with a pillow a few times, too."

"You'd never do it. You're all talk."

I grin savagely and grab her pillow, attempting to pin her to the bed. While we laugh, squeal, and grapple, her foot hits the holo projector unit and changes the channel.

Peering over her shoulder as she attempts to throttle me, I gape when I see Thrase's face on the display.

"Hold up, Lamira. Truce, already. Look at the news."

She rolls off of me, tossing the pillow to the side, and gapes at the image. I turn up the volume so we can hear more than a low drone.

"...if you're just joining us, this is a Novarian News Alert. The Interstellar Human Confederation has announced that it has lost custody of a number of domestic terrorists scheduled for execution. These fugitives are believed to be armed and should be considered highly dangerous, and the authorities have stated they may be traveling under false names. If you have any information about the whereabouts of these fugitives, please contact your local IHC consulate."

Then the display changes to show my face, as well as Lamira's. I thought this whole affair was due to my black-market smuggling and Lamira had been dragged in by mistake.

But now it's obvious something far more sinister is afoot. It's also obvious that we can't return to IHC space.

"...thank you for tuning in to Novarian News, your galactic news source."

Lamira kicks the display off the bed with a sneer. "Shut up, asshole."

CHAPTER TWENTY-FOUR

SOLAIR

Ensconced in my command seat on the bridge, I have a great view of the M'Kal Port Station. Its teardrop-shaped hull appears amidst the sea of stars as we drop out of superluminal speed.

"MPS directly ahead." Swipt spins his chair around and flashes a smile at me. "Shall I open a channel to the station and request a docking vector?"

"Proceed, Swipt. And try to get us near ring four if you can. I hate having to walk all the way down just to jam my credstick into their outdated collection console."

Grantian steps up to my side, his gaze distant and his tone contemplative. "I wonder if some of the human women might wish to disembark here? It would be simple to arrange transport back to IHC territory at such a busy port as M'Kal."

He's not wrong about that. As we vector in closer to the station, its docking rings resolve themselves to our gazes, as well as the tiny shimmering dots moving both toward and away from its central mass. Those tiny dots are actually ships, many of them much larger than the *Queen*.

"Perhaps." This idea bothers me for some reason. After the startling turn of events between me and Varia, the thought of her leaving in very short order has me both discombobulated and a little bit frustrated. "Perhaps I should speak with Varia and find out?"

Grantian nods. "That might be prudent. They should also be informed of some of the... less than savory elements and alleyways of MPS."

"Varia strikes me as someone who can take care of herself, but I'll definitely pass it along." I unfold from my seat and clap him on the shoulder. "You have the bridge."

He nods, eyes still focused on the station as it grows larger on the view screen. Just as I'm about to leave, I turn back toward him, a grin stretching my lips. "Oh, Grantian, it's come to my attention that you gifted your Durzacorp holovid projector to Varia's friend, Lamira. The same one you ranted on and on about for months, with its three trillion color array and such..."

Grantian attempts to keep his expression neutral, but the sudden stiffness in his shoulders is hard to miss. "Ahem. Well, that's only because I intend to buy an even better, newer model. Here. At the station. Today. You'll see."

He sits at the command chair and punches keys on the console, bringing up telemetry spreads that Swipt is more than capable of handling on his own. I chuckle to myself and leave him be.

I first check the mess hall but don't find Varia there. Likewise, the med bay is bereft of her presence. It would be logical to check her quarters, perhaps as even my first destination, but I'm oddly anxious about being alone with her in close confines. It's not that I don't trust myself. I'm just afraid that our tenuous peace might be dispelled if I say or do the wrong thing.

As I roam about my vessel, nodding at crewmen and moving aside for those carrying burdens, my mind drifts back to when she was warm and soft in my arms. I can't forget the taste of her lips or the way she just kind of melted her form into my own when I told her she might be mine...

I actually walk right past cargo bay nine, which is echoing with Varia's voice, before I realize I've stumbled across my quarry by accident. When I enter the room, I just catch the tail end of the conversation she's having with Fiona and Marion.

"...so that's all I've been able to glean so far. They're blaming us for a bombing on an IHC mining colony called Kaleth that I've never even heard of. The fact is, it's not safe for us to even—"

She turns at the sound of my footsteps and instantly her gaze drops to the floor before she forces it to return to my face. Her fellow *Frontier* women notice the reaction and exchange befuddled glances.

"Captain Solair." Her tone is as formal as my title, and the smile she gives me is bereft of teeth but full of anxiety. "How can I assist you?"

For a moment I can't respond because all I can think about is how she's my fated mate, but then I force myself to speak. "I..." I clear my throat and force myself to go on. I dislike this sudden distance between us. "I just wanted to inform you that we will soon be docking with M'Kal Port Station, a fairly large transit hub for this sector." I lick my suddenly dry lips before continuing. "It might be possible for some of your number to disembark here and seek transit back to the IHC territories."

Varia's face scrunches up in a grimace. I was expecting an entirely different reaction. I step forward, reaching out to touch her but pulling my hand back at the last instant.

"What's the matter? I thought that you were anxious to return home."

She heaves a heavy sigh, and runs a hand over her face.

"That may not be an option for some of us, Solair." She gestures at Fiona and herself. "It seems that whatever conspiracy put us on the *Frontier* in the first place goes deeper than we thought. A lot of the girls are facing criminal charges if they return, including me."

I had considered as much. The holovid broadcast marking Varia and what I've come to think of as her "senior staff" as terrorists has been the talk of the *Queen* today. It might be far too dangerous for any of them, truth to be told.

"Judging by the looks on your faces, I'm guessing this level of criminal activity is not something that's jogging your memory?" I raise a single brow with my question.

"No," Varia shakes her head. "None of my girls are terrorists. Simple thieves and maybe skirting the grayer areas of the law, but we don't go around killing people."

"And the human government is saying you did?"

"They think we bombed and destroyed a mining colony."

"Does anyone have family or friends who can vouch for them? Maybe spouses or children?"

"That's the thing," Varia looks around, scratching the back of her neck. "Most if not all of the girls who are awake now aren't married. And if they were married in the past, they're divorced now. The ones I've talked to don't have children and they weren't living with their parents. They were pretty much independent and on their own."

"Which means they have no character references or alibi?"

"Also, it means that no one missed them when they were gone."

A part of my brain tugs at me.

Varia may be right. There may be more to these women being on the ship than what appeared on the surface.

Fiona steps forward, holding the data pad she'd been pecking on at her side. Its screen casts an eerie glow on the floor, making sinister shadows.

"Varia? I might be able to help with at least one of our problems."

My destined mate turns toward her tech guru, brows climbing on her face in query. "Oh? I could use some good news."

"It might not help for you or me, or the rest of the 'terrorists,' given that they're expecting us to be tricky, but I have ways of securing things that aren't exactly traded upon the open market."

Varia flashes a panicked gaze over to me and then moves in close to her friend.

"Maybe don't say that quite so fucking loudly next time, Fiona."

Fiona spreads her hands and shrugs. "I had been striving for subtlety."

"You weren't striving hard enough."

"Please, ladies." They both swivel their faces in my direction, and for a moment I lose my nerve. "Ah...there's no need to fear my reaction to a little dabbling in the black market. I usually take above-board contracts, but when things are tight, I've been known to... skirt the law."

For some reason, that declaration seems to relax Varia. The tension drains from her face, and she glances over at Fiona. "Go ahead and spill your plan, I guess. It's all right."

"Okay, boss. Here's the situation. With over ten trillion estimated sapients in the galaxy, how do you know the person you're talking to is really who they say they are?"

Varia's brow furrows in confusion.

"Well, I suppose...I'd check their passport, or maybe do a retinal DNA scan?"

"Ah, but how do you know that the information provided by those things is correct?" Fiona's eyes are shining, and her manner is a trifle more eager than I'm comfortable with, considering we're talking about illegal activities. "All it takes is the right person on the right data system to change that information to whatever they want, and presto. You have a new identity."

"Fake IDs?" Varia shakes her head and frowns. "I'm not going to ask where you learned how to do this, or why, but I'm just going to point out that a fake photo isn't going to fool a DNA scanner."

Fiona chuckles and buffs her nails on her coveralls before blowing on them smugly. "All the scanner is going to do is access the galactic database. If the info in there says you are who you say you are, the scan is a nonissue."

I consider this information, rubbing my fingers across my lips. It seems like a solution that's far from foolproof. While many of the women might be able to find passage back to the IHC, it won't be their home world. And with the reason for their incarceration upon the *Frontier* in cryopods still unclear, it seems a risky proposition to drop them off on a free port as exciting as MPS can be.

"Varia?"

She pauses in her discussion with Fiona and turns her gaze upon me. "Yes?"

"I would speak to you about this matter in private. Would you be willing to join me in my quarters?"

There's only the briefest of pauses before she gestures toward the open bay door. "Very well. Lead on."

CHAPTER TWENTY-FIVE

VARIA

There's a ton of tension stretched taut in the air between me and Solair as the golden-skinned, horned Kilgari captain leads me to his private cabin.

While some of it is no doubt because he's now harboring a "known terrorist" on his ship, I believe our prior encounter is really weighing heavily on both of our minds.

I think the rest of his crew, as well as my fellow refugees from the *Frontier*, can pick up on this tension. No one interferes with our progress through the snaking corridors of the *Ancestral Queen's* beautifully decorated interior. Again I'm struck that this vessel is as much a work of art as it is a practical transport ship.

Then we turn a corner and come upon the revered short stairway that leads up to Solair's cabin. If there weren't already rumors swirling about us, there certainly will be now. I'm not sure what to make of the fact that I secretly wish I was guilty as charged, despite nothing happening the last time we were alone in there.

The door slides open, and he gestures for me to precede him into his cabin. This time I pick up a few more details, like the two-dimensional star map lovingly painted on the far wall by hand and a table full of different artifacts whose sole purpose seems to be aesthetic. While many of them are arcane, Kilgari in nature, one of them I recognize on sight because it's part of Earth history.

I pick up the roughly two-foot-long, beautifully sculpted device and peer down its length.

"A human freighter captain I sometimes drink with gifted that artifact to me." Solair moves up to stand beside me, smiling down at the device in my hand. "When I asked him its purpose, he said something that I not only believe is incorrect, but vulgar and unnecessarily crude."

My laugh makes his smile widen, and I hand him the device.

"Your suspicions are most astute. This is a sextant, a device used by ancient sailors on Earth to navigate our world's many oceans."

"I see." He peers at the sextant with new respect and then

points both his horns and his gaze at me. "I understand that your home world is nearly entirely covered in water."

"Not entirely. There was a point in our history where we didn't pay enough attention to the havoc wrought on the environment by our industry and the sea levels rose, but we joined together to change." I sigh and shake my head sadly. "I could use a little of that good old-fashioned human solidarity right now, instead of being framed for a horrific crime I did not commit."

Solair's jaw works silently for a moment, and then he moves away from me toward a waist-high brass cabinet with artful glassteel window panes. He opens one of the panes, takes out a dark red bottle, and cradles it lovingly in his large hands.

"Kilgari Nutmash Wine." Solair snags a pair of delicately tapered glasses with magnetic bases from the top of the cabinet and then moves over to sit in one of the two chairs. I sit in the opposite as he pours us each a few fingers. "Don't let the name fool you. It is as sophisticated and refined a drink as one can find this far from the galactic core."

I pick up one of the glasses and sniff the liquid within. My nose picks up notes of spice similar to Terran pepper, the hot ones at that, but there's something akin to cinnamon as well.

Solair picks up his glass as well and then clears his throat.

"Ah...I understand there is a human tradition before drinking spirits such as these. I believe you call it a cracker?"

"Cracker?" I do the translation in my head and chuckle. "Close. Toast. We call it a toast."

"I see. Shall we toast, then?"

"Um, sure." What do we toast to, though? He's just sitting there looking at me over his glass, the handsome bastard. Why am I suddenly so hot? Am I sitting on top of a heat register? "Ah... to understanding... things."

Lame. Lame with a capital L, Varia. But Solair doesn't seem to mind. We clink our glasses together, a merry sound.

"To understanding things." We each take a sip, and I'm pleasantly surprised at how good the wine tastes. It's a bit spicy, to be sure, but its low minerality and smooth finish have me thirsting for more. Solair sets his glass down and sighs before speaking.

"Varia... I am on your side. I hope you realize that. I've come to realize that I really care about what happens to you... to you and your people. So please don't get angry at what I'm about to propose."

"Oooh." I set my glass down too. "I see. I can offer you no promises, Solair, but I'm willing to hear you out in any event."

"That's fair enough. I've been thinking it might be best if none of your number disembark at M'Kal station. Given how little we know of the circumstances of your even being in our space, it seems prudent to remain cautious."

I'm a bit taken aback, both by how diplomatically he phrased his plea and how sincere it sounds. I think I need a little more wine before I respond and lift my glass for another sip.

"Well, I'm not mad." I set the glass down on its heavy base and give him a small smile. "I'd been thinking much the same thing. Even those of us without warrants out on our heads could be at high risk."

My heart starts beating faster and my palms go sweaty, but it's not from the tiny amount of wine I've had. I'm about to ask Solair a huge favor, one that means putting a great imposition upon him and his ship.

"Captain Solair—"

"Please, Varia. I've already told you formality is a barrier, and I want no barriers between us. Especially with what transpired between us last night. Call me Solair."

I don't want to read too much into his "no barriers" policy at the moment because I'm distracted enough by his mere presence and this is important.

"Very well. Do you think the women and I could remain on board the *Ancestral Queen*, just for a while? I know it's an imposition, but we don't have many options, and even fewer friends in this region of space."

Solair leans back in his chair and I get the feeling he was about half expecting me to make this request. He doesn't seem shocked or angry, but he's definitely a bit anxious.

"I think that we can arrange that, Varia, but there may be some... limitations."

If Solair and his crew had not been so respectful and generous during our stay, I would read something really creepy into that statement. As it is, it still makes me nervous. "That sounds logical enough. Go ahead. Hit me with these limitations."

Solair sips his wine and then leans forward, elbows on top of his long thighs. "This vessel is as sound as they come, but its age and technology require constant maintenance. I'm sure you've noticed my crew are rarely idle. This is as much a testament to necessity as work ethic. With one hundred and seven new passengers, that burden will only increase upon my crew, so much so that they may not be able to maintain ship systems properly."

I lean forward as well, my palms pressed together between my thighs. I can't stop bouncing my knees, a nervous habit I've never quite been able to eliminate.

"Stop beating around the bush, Solair. I smell what you're cooking."

He blinks his golden eyes several times before responding. "You do?'

"Sure. You want us to help with the work to be done on the *Queen*. I think it's a splendid idea. Between Thrase and your man Nicari, more able-bodied crew are being revived every day. A lot of us have skills that I'm sure you can put to good use, and I can't think of anyone who's not willing to do their part, especially after you've been so generous to us." I sigh and stare at my folded hands. "I know I've been brusque and short tempered, but don't think for a moment I don't appreciate what you've done for me... for us, Solair."

His hands move into my point of view, enveloping my own. Solair's touch is warm and comforting and I raise my gaze to meet his.

A long moment passes, with the two of us just staring at each other. Then he leans in for a kiss and I lift my chin to accept it. His taste mingles with the spice of the wine, a heady mix that has my blood rushing through my ears.

Somehow, we're standing, moving across the room in a molten clench until he lays me down gently on his bed. I stare up at him through half-lidded eyes as he tugs at my clothing, slowly exposing my flesh to his fiery gaze.

"You're so beautiful, Varia..." His breath is hot in my ear and then on my neck as he trails kisses across my sensitive skin. I moan softly when he carefully kisses each of my breasts in turn before moving down past my navel, his hands finishing the task of removing my trousers.

One of his horns scrapes along my ribs as he nuzzles between my thighs, seeming to exult in the moist, musky embrace of my nether lips. My mouth flies open, and my hands clutch at the back of his head as he plies his nimble tongue and lips all over my pussy, exploring it millimeter by millimeter.

Solair's gaze snaps up to meet my own, the intensity in his golden orbs hotter than a blue star. His hands caress the curve of my hips as he continues to lap greedily at me. I don't know if it's all the tension or if I'm just really that into him, but soon the walls of his well-furnished cabin echo with my screams of climax.

For someone who doesn't spend much time around women, he seems to know his way around our bodies quite well...

CHAPTER TWENTY-SIX

SOLAIR

The more she moans, the more I want her.

The more she screams, the more I need her.

Draping one arm over her waist, I pin her against the mattress as I continue ravaging her with my tongue. I caress her drenched inner lips, enjoying the way her feminine flavor coils itself around every single rational thought I have, and it doesn't take long before I have my lips wrapped around her pleasure bud.

"That feels so..." she trails off, her voice turning into a quivering moan. Reaching down, she grabs me by the horns and pulls me toward her, trapping me in as place as she moves her hips. She does it in an almost desperate manner, her entire body emanating a scorching heat. Eager to subdue this desperation of hers, I redouble my efforts, whipping at her clit until her moans start to turn into full-blown screaming. Again.

Her voice, bright and sweet, is all it takes for me to let go of my rational mind. Pure and unbridled instinct takes its place, and I let lust take over me. Devouring her with the same ferocity a predator would devour its prey, I drive her toward the edge of pleasure's cliff, but I hold on before giving her one final push.

Patience, they say, is a virtue.

Gently, I start twirling my tongue around her clit as I press two fingers against her entrance. I feel her slick outer lips under my fingertips, liquid desire coating her sensitive skin, and I take my time as I ease my fingers in. I curl them upward like a hook, stretching her inner walls as I go, and I only stop when I feel the spot I was looking for. Pressing hard against that hidden cavern inside of her, only then do I unleash hell upon her body.

"I think I'm gonna—"

She doesn't get to finish her sentence.

Her voice dips into a low growl, one brimming with ecstasy, and she arches her back. She digs her heels into the mattress, pushing her wetness against my mouth, and grips my horns so tightly that it almost seems like she wants to rip them off my head.

Tiny spasms take over her inner lips as she finally explodes, her entire body turning into a furnace. Swaying her hips from side to side, she rides that wave of pleasure until it finally starts to recede, the echo of her moans and screams still bouncing inside my skull. This was even better than I assumed it would be. And the best part? We're just getting started.

Pulling back from her, I let my eyes roam up her naked body until I'm looking into her eyes. It's not an easy task. Her curves seem to demand my attention, the perfection of her rosy nipples like a beacon, but I still manage to hold her gaze all the same. It's worth it. Her face has been taken over by an expression of pure bliss and, even though I don't know how that's possible, she looks even more beautiful now. Her lips are curled into a lazy smile, her eyelids fluttering gently as she returns my gaze, and stray locks of her disheveled hair tumble over her face.

"What are you looking at?" she teases me, her voice mellow and tender. Pushing herself off the mattress with her elbows, she reaches for me with one hand and places two fingers under my chin. She pulls me up and toward her, a delirious smile dawning on her lips, and then she leans in. Her mouth comes crashing down on mine, and my heart picks up the pace once I feel the velvety texture of her lips.

She doesn't rush our kiss. Taking her time, she nibbles on my bottom lip and then uses the tip of her tongue to lick them dry, tasting herself on me. As she does it, she lays one hand on my chest and allows it to wander down to my waist. Quick to find my belt, she unbuckles it with one fast movement and then pulls it free from its loops.

"You have no idea how much I want you right now," she whispers against my lips. Resting my forehead against hers, I look straight into her eyes and let a wicked grin spread across my lips.

"Actually, I think I have an idea," I say, taking one hand between her legs and flattening my palm against her wetness. She opens her mouth to let a soft moan escape and then something breaks inside her. All the patience and gentleness melts away from her, and in its place rises unbridled lust.

Dropping my belt to the floor, she turns her hand around and, spreading her fingers wide, presses it between my legs. I become even harder than I already was, my two cocks throbbing viciously against her fingers. Spurred by that, she takes her other hand and then grips both my erections over the fabric of my trousers.

"Is this for me?" she asks me, that sweet madness of desire adding a perfect little twang to her voice. "All of it?"

"It's all yours," I reply, keeping my eyes on hers as I pull my shirt over my head. Her eyes widen for a moment as they trace the contour of my pecs and abs, taking in every ridge and groove of my muscles. She tightens her fingers around my hardness so much that I can't help but groan.

"I like the sound of that." She lets go of me, but only momentarily. Hooking her fingers on the hem of my pants, she pulls them down my legs with one hard yank. Instead of rushing it all, she pauses before giving my underwear the same treatment. With slow but deliberate movements, she uses her fingers to trace the contour of my erect cocks over the fabric, and only then does she pull down the remaining layer of clothing between the two of us.

My hard cocks spring free to salute her at once.

Turning her wrists around, she doesn't hesitate before she grips them both by their roots. When she looks down to appreciate my size, I notice a lustful mad glint in her eyes, but I don't have the time to dwell on it. She starts moving her hands up and down my length right away, stroking me in the most perfect of manners. Her strokes alternate between harsh and delicate, and I can't help but admire the way she's blending such distinct rhythms into the same movement. It shouldn't be possible for a woman to inflict this much pleasure using nothing but her hands but...well, here we are.

Varia is different.

She's better.

"I need to have you," I find myself saying, the words leaving my mouth before I can even process what I just said. This woman is making me feel something I haven't felt before. Whatever this is, it goes beyond the lust of the flesh. In a way, it's almost as if my soul wants to devour hers. I'm on the verge of losing all fucking control, and the crazy part is that with her I really want to lose it all.

"I'm right here," she whispers, pressing her lips against my ear. "If you need me, take me."

She doesn't need to offer twice.

I push her down onto the mattress and climb on top of her. Grabbing her by the wrists, I pin her hands down beside her head and look into her eyes. My breath catches in my throat as she returns my gaze and, for a moment, neither of us says a damn thing. We don't need to. Right now, our bodies are doing the talking.

"I've never been with anyone like you," she whispers softly, dragging her teeth across my bottom lip. It doesn't take a genius to know what she's talking about. After all, not all species are lucky enough to be as well-equipped as the Kilgari are when it comes to sex.

"You don't have to worry," I say, cupping her face with one hand. "I'll be gentle."

Slowly, I lower my body over hers and let one of my cocks

rest against her entrance, her soft inner lips wrapping themselves around its tip. As for the other, I let it rest directly above her wetness, my hardness pressed right against her clit. I take my time as I ease myself in, allowing my thickness to stretch her inner walls. As promised, I rein myself in, doing my best to remain gentle. It's harder than I anticipated. I watch as her eyes roll in their orbits, her eyelids fluttering with excitement. I have to make a very conscious effort to restrain myself.

"How are you fee—?" I start to ask, but Varia silences me pretty quickly. She places both her hands on my naked chest and digs her fingernails into my skin.

"Shut up and fuck me," she growls.

Not exactly the answer I was expecting, but I can work with it.

Finally taking the leash off my desire, I thrust, enjoying the way my entire length ravages the sweet tightness of her body. My second cock moves up and down the mound above her pussy, its shaft keeping a steady pressure on her clit, and that seems to please her. She looks down her own body, curiosity etched on her face, and her eyes widen as takes in all the action between her legs.

"This is insane," she breathes out, and for a moment it almost seems like she's going to laugh. She doesn't. Instead, she places her hands beside her and bunches up the sheets, every single muscle on her body tensing up.

Going faster and faster, each passing second making me even more delirious with lust, I ravage her in a way I've never experienced before. She was right when she said this is insane. It really is. I never thought I'd have a woman, especially one like her, all to myself. If that's not insane, I don't know what is.

Cradling her head with one hand, I look straight into her eyes until I simply can't take it anymore, every fiber of my being aching for release. I resist the urge to explode for a while, and my resolve only starts to crumble once I finally realize I've claimed her. No matter what happens in the future, she'll never forget about the Kilgari that made her body his. She'll never forget about me. As if her own body senses the whirlwind of emotions going inside me, her inner walls suddenly tighten around my hardness like a vise, and I have no choice but to surrender to the inevitable.

We explode at the same time, sweet hellfire consuming us both.

Her moans of ecstasy fill the entire room as my cocks throb almost too desperately, my seed filling her tightness up and spilling onto her belly at the same time. She looks down as it happens, fascinated, and the scene makes her moan even louder.

Only when that tidal wave of pleasure starts to recede does she look away, and that's when she collapses on top of the mattress, completely spent. Her chest rises and falls at an urgent pace, and she places the back of her right hand over her forehead.

"This was—"

"Perfect," I cut her short. "This was absolutely perfect."

And it was.

It really was.

CHAPTER TWENTY-SEVEN

VARIA

"Where exactly do you think you're going?"

Solair moves to push himself off of me, but I lace my legs around his waist and keep him in place. Now that I've had a taste, there's no way I'm letting go of him so easily, and that's precisely what I tell him. His eyes widen with surprise, but they quickly light up with lust once more.

"Aren't you tired?" The tone of his voice tells me he already knows the answer.

"Are you?" I throw back at him, and a grin takes over his lips. The cock inside me hardens again, and I find myself returning his grin. "That's what I thought." Sliding one hand down my chest, I reach for his second cock; I lay my fingers on top of it and press it down, pushing his flesh against my clit.

"You're one of a kind, Varia," he whispers, slowly rocking his hips against mine as he builds a gentle rhythm. He seems aware that my body is way more sensitive now, but he doesn't let that stop him. His pace keeps increasing with each passing second, and it doesn't take long before he's ravaging me with the same intensity from before, his eyes never leaving mine as he thrusts. "Where have you been all my life?"

"I could ask you the same question." Placing both my hands on his face, I raise my head and crush my mouth against his, allowing our tongues to dance and wrestle in a frenzied way. Tightening my legs around him, I twist my hips around and force him to roll to the side. Even though his body is far more imposing than mine, he allows me to do it all the same, and I quickly find myself on top of him.

Grinning like a madwoman, I take over our little dance, riding him so intensely that it's only a matter of time until my muscles start complaining from the effort. Not that I pay these complaints any heed. The exhaustion I'm feeling is as sweet as the pleasure he has unleashed on my body, and it does nothing to stop me.

"You're so tight," he tells me, the lines on his face deepening as I start riding him even harder than before. I open my mouth to respond, but I don't have the strength to do it. Instead, I just use my inner walls to give his hardness a firm squeeze, the surprised look on his face almost making me laugh.

"And I'm full of surprises," I tease him, running my hands up my body until they're cupping my breasts. I keep looking at him as I play with my own body, my fingers softly massaging my hard nipples, and that seems to fuel the hellfire of lust burning inside of him. Whatever surprises I might have, he wants every single one of them.

Matching my movements, he thrusts upward, burying his cock so deeply inside me that I can't stop myself from gasping. Reacting instinctively, I reach down with one hand and grip his second cock, stroking it so frantically that pain shoots up from my wrist to my elbow. He's still slick from his own juices, so my fingers glide easily over his entire length, making my movements seem frenzied and out of control.

"You're driving me fucking insane," he growls all of a sudden and, before I can do anything to stop him, he sits up on the mattress and places both hands on my backside. He pulls me against him, trapping his second cock between us, and I throw my arms over his shoulders as I kiss him again. Locked in such a tight embrace, we settle into a more forgiving rhythm, our two bodies swaying back and forth at a smooth tempo.

Despite the gentleness of our new rhythm, the fire inside continues to grow. As we remain trapped in that sweet cadence, my insides turn into a veritable furnace, and this time my inner walls tighten up around Solair's cock on their own. I bite on his bottom lip as I come, my whole body tensing up without warning. I push myself against him with all that I have, forcing him to stop moving, and I let pleasure wash all over me.

I don't move for a few seconds, but that moment of stillness seems to stretch endlessly. I just let my breathing match Solair's and open my eyes lazily so I can take in the blissful expression on his face. I make note of each line and detail, from his strong chin to the strength and kindness in his eyes, and I engrave it all on my mind. No matter what happens, I don't want to forget this moment. I want to remember it for the rest of my days.

"You're not done. Are you?" I release a soft chuckle and rest my forehead against his. I still feel the throb of his two cocks, one inside me and the other pressed against my stomach, and that's all I need to know that he's far from being done.

"How did you know?" he asks me with a chuckle of his own. Tenderly, he pushes me off of him, and I sit down on the mattress. He goes up to his knees, allowing his smile to turn into a thin line, and then all kindness melts out from his eyes as his predatory gaze returns. "I don't want this to end, Varia. What I'm feeling right now is not even a want... it's a need."

I give him a teasing smile. "If you need something, why don't you come and take it?"

He responds by closing on me ferociously.

Grabbing me by the hips, he turns me around until I'm lying on my stomach and then forces me to push my ass up. It doesn't take a genius to know what he wants, and I'm more than willing to give it to him. Going up on all fours, I wiggle my backside at him, and then my breath catches in my throat as he presses his body against mine.

One of his cocks pushes its way past my inner lips easily, and I groan as I feel its thickness stretching me widely once more. The other lodges itself between my ass cheeks, its harsh throb against my entrance making me want so much more than what I'm getting right now. Still, I have to take it slow. Solair isn't what I'd call human-sized, and I have to take things slowly if I want to be able to walk after this encounter.

Moaning, I start thrusting back against him, and he's quick to respond to my movements. His thighs slap my ass cheeks over and over again until the sound of flesh on flesh fills the entire room. I swear it's the most perfect sound I've ever heard in my entire life. We remain locked in our frantic embrace until my moans and his groans have blended with the sounds of our bodies clashing; locks of hair are plastered to my forehead, beads of sweat rolling down my face, and I feel on the verge of collapsing. And yet...

I want so much more.

"Harder," I find myself saying, repeating that word over and over again until I'm screaming it out at the top of my lungs. Not one to hesitate, he gives me exactly what I'm asking of him, ravaging me in such a way that I can't help but think I'm having an out-of-body experience. Ecstasy is whipping at both my body and soul and, by everything that is sacred, it truly feels like we're at the center of the universe, all of it spinning around us.

When we finally surrender to the inevitable, our bodies in complete synch, a bright flash of light explodes behind my shut eyelids. I remain perfectly still as Solair offers me all of his seed, my body his for the taking, and I only move once my muscles finally reach the breaking point. I collapse on the bed, completely spent, and I don't even look to the side as I feel the mattress shifting under Solair's weight.

For a moment, there's silence, our ragged breathing the only sound in the room. Then, gently, he reaches for me and brushes one finger against my spine, tracing its length in a tender way. He takes his finger all the way up to my neck, and then goes down my jaw until he's touching my lips. Slowly, I turn around so I'm facing him, my eyes meeting his. I want to say a lot of things right now, but I don't. I just take his hand and smile.

After all, some things don't need to be said.

CHAPTER TWENTY-EIGHT

Varia

M'Kal station features a large dome with numerous curving glassteel panels, allowing a view of the sea of stars and the different merchant ships as they drift to and fro across the starscape. I find that my gaze keeps drawing up toward its more than fifty-foot height. The amount of engineering that had to go into building must have been staggering. I can't find much practical purpose to such a high, vaulted ceiling, other than eliminating the normally claustrophobic feel of space stations.

Walking abreast of me, Solair turns a smile my way.

"Amazing. Isn't it? Many of the bas reliefs were carved by the same artist who worked on the *Queen*."

"It is amazing. Both in scale and beauty." I return his smile and feel that particular tickle in my belly when I'm into someone and the feeling is mutual.

Into someone. That's the barest way to describe my feelings. The time I spent with Solair in his cabin was sweet and sensual, and I found it easy to let go and simply enjoy being with him. Things have definitely changed between us, for the better, but there's still some things to work out. But now, for the first time since we met, working them out seems not only possible, but simple.

Behind us, members of Solair's crew and a team of women handpicked by Marion, follow in our wake. The busy port has many sapient species I'm not directly familiar with, members of the League who rarely interfere with the war-torn regions of the galaxy.

The League has studiously remained neutral in the long, brutal war between the Ataxian Coalition and the Trident Alliance. I'm a bit worried I'm dragging Solair toward the conflict that he never had any part of by asking him to harbor IHC fugitives on his ship. It weighs on my conscience, but it's a burden eased by the gentle laughter of my alien lover, as well as his deft and sensitive touch.

God, I'm acting like a giddy schoolgirl. I thought I'd left such frivolity behind when I joined the IHC Marines at sixteen, but here I am right back in it. Solair makes me feel it's okay to be both strong and vulnerable at the same time, and I owe him so much for that.

"You seem troubled."

I shake my head and give his hand a squeeze. "I'm always troubled, but don't take it personally. I'm glad you're here with me."

"I am as well."

We head around the circumference of the docking ring, gradually working our way to the admin office. Solair intends to pay our docking fee before heading down a ring to negotiate with a merchant he's worked with before.

"So tell me about this Hudd person we're going to meet later."

Solair cocks an eyebrow at me, and his lips stretch in an easy grin. "He's a sneaky bastard, a shrewd negotiator, and has a penchant for the dramatic. You'll like him."

"So you say. If he can help us find the things on Marion's list, I'll hug the guy."

"A side hug only, I hope." He chuckles, belying the jealous words he spoke with his tone and manner. "I'm certain that if Hudd can't help us directly, he'll be more than happy to point us in the right direction, for an only marginally exorbitant finder's fee."

"If this guy's such a mensch, why do business with him at all?"

Solair shrugs. "For a merchant who calls M'Kal station home, he's a paradigm of virtue. Also, even if he's a bit persnickety, he does find fantastic bargains. For an operation such as ours, men like him are a necessary evil, and he's far less evil than most."

When we get to the admin office, there's a short line to wait in. Solair directs Kintar to take our entourage—and their fully laden hover sleds of goods—down to the merchant ring in preparation of our transactions with this Hudd character.

Solair glances over at me as we shuffle forward in line. "I can't stop thinking about our encounter in my quarters."

"Encounter?" I shoot him a teasing smile. "Is that a euphemism for the fact that we fu   "

"Made love? Indeed."

I chuckle and entwine my arm with his. Right now, in this instant, all of my problems don't seem so big or scary. Maybe that's what finding your person is all about?

At last, we reach the front of the line and Solair jams his cred stick into the automated console.

"Tonnage...trajectory...oh come on, why does it matter how many cargo bays I have? Four thousand creds? You leeches."

I hide my laugh behind my hand as he punches in the data. Everyone keeps talking about Solair's sense of humor, but this is the first real evidence I've seen of it. I guess we have been going at it pretty hard... well, we were going at it pretty hard in his cabin, but in a much different context.

Once the docking fee has been paid—amid a constant storm of grumbling about inflation and the effects of the distant war—we take the lift down the center spoke of the M'Kal station and arrive on the slightly slimmer merchant ring. The smells of the market hit my nostrils before the doors even slide all the way open.

I gape at the sight of hundreds of sapients engaging in negotiations, carefully squeezing produce, and moving stacks of cargo to and fro. It's the best tangible example of controlled chaos I've ever seen. While it's impossible to take in all of the sights and sounds at once, no one seems to be getting in each other's way, though more than a few hot arguments spike up.

"Come, I think I see our people." Solair grasps my hand and we move single file through the milling throng. My head is on a swivel, taking in the various sensual delights even as he tugs me inexorably forward. I've been to a lot of ports and I consider myself to be pretty jaded, but the color and tumult of the M'Kal station is a few notches above the mundane.

We reach what first appears as a seller's booth, but then it resolves itself into the open cargo bay of a docked vessel. A Kilgari male stands with his arms akimbo, a half grin creasing his wizened features as Solair and I stride up to join Marion and the others.

This must be Hudd, and I can see that Solair did not undersell him, at least from what I can glean from his appearance. Hudd wears a wide-brimmed cap with something between a feather and a giant reptile scale stuck in its gold band. The loose blouse adorning his torso features a plunging v-neck to display his chiseled chest, and a midnight blue cloak shimmers on his broad shoulders. This guy takes peacocking to a higher level. Each of his arms jangles with dozens of bracelets, and a cigar juts from between his lean fingers.

"Oh, just when I thought my day couldn't get any worse. It's you."

Solair grins and moves up to stand before Hudd. "Don't pretend like I haven't made you a much more financially stable male, Hudd. You look forward to seeing my gorgeous face in your shopfront."

Hudd puffs on his cigar and arches an eyebrow high on his golden-skinned face. I notice that like Kintar his horns are filed down to mere nubs.

"Is that what you think? Please. Every time you come around your miserly ways keep me out of my wife's bed. She has seven other husbands, you know, and they don't have to negotiate with a cheapskate privateer like you."

"I would think a man of your talents would see it as a challenge."

I hide my smile behind my hand. It's obvious to me that Solair and Hudd have a grudging respect for each other, and all this word play lacks any serious venom.

"Would you now? That's not the sort of challenge I like to engage in." Hudd sighs and leans his hands on the low metal panel he uses as a counter. "All right, Solair. Let's stop pretending like we're friends and get down to it."

"I would never dream of pretending to be friends with you, Hudd. I wouldn't want to hurt my reputation."

"Your reputation is already ruined because you pay so very little for goods I have spent much to acquire. I assume you want the usual assortment?"

Solair nods, crossing his arms over his chest. "You assume correctly. For once."

"Well, I don't know if you pay much attention to current events..."

"As much as anyone, I suppose."

"How droll. Anyway, given the situation on Armstrong, and the sudden reemergence of the Reaper threat from the Badlands, everyone's tightening their grip on their credsticks. People are scared. I'm going to have to hit you up for a twenty percent increase in my usual commission."

"Twenty percent?" Solair scoffs, his golden-skinned face creasing. "Come on, Hudd. A smart guy like you wouldn't let current events pry even a single, solitary cred out of your account. You have to be able to do better than that. Twelve percent."

"Twelve?" Now it's Hudd's turn to scoff. "You're breaking my balls, Solair."

"That's a bigger commission than you got last time."

"True, in the way that a Vakutan is bigger than a Shorcu, which is to say not by much. Eighteen percent, you stingy bastard, and damn you for my upcoming blue balls."

"Your marital affairs are of no concern to me, Hudd. Fifteen percent." Solair crosses his arms over his chest. "Final offer."

Hudd glares for a long time, but then he breaks into laughter and holds out his hand, palm facing outward. Solair presses his own palm against it, and they do a sort of ritualistic circling with them, which I assume seals their bargain.

First his astonishingly gentle touch in the bedroom, and now this humorous side emerges. I'm beginning to think I might be falling in love with this golden-skinned, horned rogue.

And the idea does not frighten me nearly as much as it should.

CHAPTER TWENTY-NINE

SOLAIR

As Varia, Kintar, Marion, and our bearers look on, I begin the inspection of the cargo I gleaned from Hudd's tight, clutching fingers. The deal we made is fair, to be sure, but I was hoping it would be a little fairer for me, if you catch my meaning.

The cargo awaits my scrutinizing gaze on four separate hover sleds, each covered with a shiny silver tarp pinned to the sled via taut white twine. Most of them are about waist height, though one narrow container is over seven feet tall. I untie the complicated knot securing the tarp on the first bin and fling it aside, revealing what lies within.

"Well, at least this cargo is something I recognize."

I flash a grin at Varia before moving on to the next crate. When I fling the cover off, a crate full of roughly spheroid, hand-sized chrome devices is revealed. They have numerous knobs and protrusions, but none of them look quite the same. Varia starts to reach into the bin, but stops herself.

"Okay to touch?" she glances at me, eyebrows raised in question. "Not going to boil my hands off or anything right?"

"No, those you may safely touch."

Varia reaches in and plucks one of the devices from the crate. Fiona moves over next to me and picks one up as well, her eyes as wide as dinner plates.

"What are they?"

I turn to Varia's friend and tech expert. "They are known as gophormanchu. They were created by the famous tabletop game designer Xagy Xylax a decade ago."

Fiona twists one of the oblong protrusions, and it sinks into the sphere's mass. The others along its surface shift and flow like water. "This has nanotech written all over it." She looks over to me, her brows climbing her face. "What does it do?"

I shrug. "No one knows. There have been entire volumes of the Encyclopedia Galactica holonet edition written about possible uses. Some believe it is a harmless but challenging puzzle. Others think they might be more insidious. All I know is that they're all the rage in the Zeffron system and we stand to make a tidy profit."

Varia places her device back in the bin but Fiona turns toward me, her eyes growing large and her lips trembling as if near tears.

"What—what are you doing?'

Varia laughs and slips her hand around my waist. "She's using an ancient Terran mind control technique called 'puppy dog eyes' so you'll let her keep that gopher —gokart—go..."

"Gophormanchu."

"Whatever."

I stare nervously at Fiona and lick my suddenly dry lips. "Why do I suddenly feel so anxious? This—this sorcery must end. Tell her to stop."

Varia shrugs her shoulders helplessly. "Have you ever tried to convince Fi to change her mind? You're better off asking space not to be cold. If I were you, I'd just let her have it and save yourself the torment."

"Fiona, you may take it with my blessing."

Fiona's face instantly morphs into a wide smile. "Thank you." Then she stares intently at the device as she twists it to and fro. "You will surrender your secrets unto me, bwah ha ha."

"All right, crew, let's get this cargo loaded. Varia, did your people get everything you need?"

"For now, Solair. Ilya already loaded it onto your ship."

"Then let's make haste. Time is creds."

Once our cargo has been loaded onto the *Queen*, I head up to the bridge for a meeting with my senior staff, as is customary. While we could speak over comms, I like getting the whole group together in person on a regular basis. I think it helps build camaraderie, among other benefits.

"Captain on the bridge," snaps Grantian. I slide into my seat and take in the room with my gaze.

"All right, our next stop is the Zeffron system..."

"As usual," interjects Lokyer.

"—and we've got the cargo from Hudd. Who wants to go first on their status report?"

Montier steps forward, his legs stiff with anger. "I'll go first, all right. You have to do something about the women. That—that Ilya greaser is always screwing with my settings, second guessing everything I do. I can't work under these conditions."

Swipt lets out a sharp bark of laughter.

"But let me ask you, Montier—have any of her modifications been wrong?"

Montier sputters a bit, trying to maintain some of his dignity. "That—that's beside the point. Just because you stare at her gluteus muscles when you think no one is watching doesn't mean you have to stick up for her."

Zander purses his lips, fingers drumming on his tactical console.

"What I think Montier is trying to get at is that we're all a little anxious about integrating the women from the *Frontier* into our crew."

Kintar sneers at him from across the bridge. "What would you have us do, cast them to the four solar winds?"

"No, of course not." Zander holds his hands up in mock defense. "I don't mean any disrespect, Kintar. I know you and what's-her-name have grown close. And I like them, I really do. The ship seems more... sunny now."

Everyone nods in agreement, but then Zander continues. "But that being said, you can't just smash a hover car and a shuttle together and expect the resulting mess to work like a shuttle. It takes time, and deliberate action, to bring two different parts into a cohesive whole."

Grantian clears his throat, and we all turn toward him. "And another matter...we were wondering, just who are we supposed to listen to? You or Varia?"

"Well, me..." my voice trails off because I realize that if Varia is to remain on the *Queen* as my mate, it will require a great deal of adjustment—some easier to make than others. "Thank you, gentlemen. You've given me a great deal to think about, and I promise you we're going to make this work. Dismissed."

As those not on active bridge duty file out of the door, I rest my chin in my hand and ponder our future on the *Queen*. No matter that Varia and I have worked out most of our issues, I still don't see her being comfortable with me ordering the *Frontier* women around as if they were my own crew.

Perhaps we could share leadership? Co-captainships are rare but not unheard of. My father was co-captain of a Vakutan freighter before he earned enough to buy the *Queen*. But it's not something I have ever personally done.

And besides, I'm not really sure I want a co-captain.

CHAPTER THIRTY

VARIA

Now that Solair and I have worked out our future on the ship—more or less—I decide it's time to check in with the rest of my "crew" and see how they fare.

Solair is busy in a meeting with his senior staff on the bridge, so now seems the perfect time to get this done. Without the big boss Kilgari around, I might get more honest responses from the women.

The first place I check for Thrase is the med bay, but I don't see either her or Doctor Nicari within. A woman is resting in one of the beds, a recent release from the cryopods, but I don't want to disturb her with queries.

Instead, I check the observation deck and that's where I find the professor. She's ensconced against the far wall, back resting against a copper hued oblong cushion. I can see the top of her head above the data pad she holds in front of her face, and judging from the movement, she's aware of my entry.

But as I stride toward her, she continues to hide behind her pad, causing me some consternation.

"Thrase?" I tilt my head to the side in a vain attempt to see around the pad. I don't know why she's holding it so close to her face. That has to make it hard to read. "Hello? Are you alive back there?"

Thrase pulls the pad away from her face and rolls her eyes to the ceiling.

"For the love of Kepler, Varia." Her tone is rife with indignation. "Can't a woman engage in some digitally assisted nostril excavation in peace?"

"Digitally..." I shake my head. "I don't understand, but if you're busy I can come back later."

I turn to leave, but Thrase shakes her head and snags my sleeve.

"No, it's fine. I'm finished with my very private and also very revolting task. How can I assist you?"

"It's nothing much, I just wanted to check in and see how

you're settling in here on the *Queen*. We'll be staying for a while, so I'm checking in on everyone."

Thrase pushes her glasses up higher on her nose and fixes me with an inscrutable gaze. "Settling in. What a quaint way to put it. Do you know how hard it is to make quantum entanglement architecture without a decent matter collider? The Kilgari are using tech from before I was born. It's like I've been sent back to prehistoric times."

I try—and fail—to keep a smile off my face at her typical rantings. "What I was getting at was whether you're comfortable and your needs are being met... that sort of thing."

"Oh." She purses her lips and scowls. "I suppose my biological imperatives are suitably satisfied, though sometimes it is a trifle annoying to have to wait in line for the sanitation facilities."

"Long lines for the bathroom is one of the things Solair and I are working on. Please try to be patient, and spread the word that we're on it. Okay?"

"You sound as if I'm some sort of busybody or gossip, but very well. I will acquiesce to your request."

"Thank you." I turn to leave but then pause at the door leading out into the corridor. "Oh, and don't wipe your boogers on Solair's cushions."

I leave her gaping and head deeper into the ship,

chuckling to myself. My next target is Ilya, and I don't have to wonder where she'll be—either in the mess hall or in the engine room. I'm not sure when or if she sleeps. If I threw a squirrel and an entire pot of espresso into a blender it would come out Ilya.

On my way to the engine room, I nearly bump into Fiona. She's got her eyes transfixed upon the gophormanchu device in her hands as she struggles to unravel its mystery. "Whoa. Sorry, Varia."

"No worries." I rub at the spot on my forearm where one of the device's protrusions jabbed me. "Listen, I've been speaking to people about how they're settling in on the *Queen*, given that we're going to be staying a while. Do you have any concerns?"

Her face twists into a sneer. "Oh, I can get used to waiting in line for the vacuum tube, or having to make do with these artistic forgeries of tools the Kilgari favor, but the next time that Jax guy yells at me for hacking the lock on his pantry..."

"Settle down, Fi. Why are you hacking the lock on his pantry in the first place?"

"You know I've got a speedy metabolism. Sometimes a girl needs a nosh in the dead of the night. I'm a grown adult. I should be able to get food whenever I want."

I try to restrain a smile and keep my tone reassuring, but it's hard. "Well, I'm fairly certain Jax is just doing his job and trying to make sure our provisions last until the next time we can resupply, but I can ask Solair to talk to him if you like."

"Oh, I like."

Apparently, she doesn't have any other major issues because she returns her attention to the puzzle and heads off down the corridor. Since the quarters I share with Lamira and Thrase are sort of on the way to the engine room where I expect to find Ilya, I stop there first and find Lamira sitting cross-legged on her bed, skillfully finishing up a needlepoint project.

"That's great work, Lamira."

She looks up and smiles, splaying the fabric on the bed so I can see it fully. "I didn't get a very good look at the *Queen* from the outside, so I'm working from a possibly flawed memory."

"Looks accurate to me. But I'm surprised to find you doing handicrafts. Didn't you want to finish watching *As the Galaxy Churns?*"

"That? I'm through with it. Binged the entire new season in one go. Besides, you know I like to keep my hands busy."

I smile at her and gesture toward the door. "I'm about to head down to speak with Ilya, hopefully. Did you want to come along?"

"Nah, I'm good here. Tell her I said hello."

I head toward the exit, but Lamira calls out at the last moment.

"Hey, Varia?"

Turning back to her, I arch my eyebrow in query. "What's up?"

"Um... since you're probably going to be sleeping in Solair's quarters from now on, can I have your blanket?"

I wipe my hand across my face and sigh. "That's not... nothing is settled... I'm just going to leave."

How many people know? Shit, probably everyone. There're no secrets on a ship this crowded, and it's not like Solair and I have been subtle ever since we made our connection official between us.

When I get to engineering, Ilya has been replaced by a woman-sized, Ilya-shaped oozing mass of black tar. Just as I enter the portal, two Kilgari blast her with sonic pressure hoses. Her eyes are squeezed shut as if from strain, but her mouth stretches in a wide grin.

Gradually, they remove the oil coating until Ilya resembles her old self.

"Whoo hoo." She pulls plugs out of her ears and laughs. "Like being front row at a Burning Blood concert."

"I can see that you're settling in just fine," I drawl. "Did you have any concerns about integrating onto the ship?"

"The lines for the bathrooms are too long and Montier doesn't know a phase flux inducer coil from a reverse thruster carbonation unit. Honestly, I don't know how this overly ornate relic stays in the air."

"Ilya, I respect your abilities, but Montier is the chief engineer and you're kind of in his wheelhouse—or playpen, if you'd prefer."

"Well, this playpen is headed for disaster. You heard it here first."

The Kilgari don't seem offended by her diatribe, so I decide to let it go for now. "Did you have any other concerns not related to the devices in this room?"

"Just that the lines for the..."

"I know. I know. We're working on it."

I leave her to her own devices—not to mention Montier's —and exit engineering, lost in my own thoughts.

While there's obviously a lot of work to be done to fully prepare the *Queen* for so many new crew members, it seems to me like overall everyone is happy to be here. That's a big relief for me, but it doesn't mean my work is finished. Far from it.

My work. I shake my head in denial. No, it's our work

now—mine and Solair's. I need to get together with him so we can work out all of these logistical issues.

If we can't work together as a cohesive unit, and be utterly transparent while we do it, both the *Frontier* women and the Kilgari crew will suffer. There's no fucking this up. It has to be done right.

I just hope we're up to the challenge.

CHAPTER THIRTY-ONE

Solair

A time-honored tradition among star captains is to walk the ship when their mind is troubled. My father taught me this long ago, when I was still quite young. Not only does the exercise tend to stimulate the brain, but it's also a good way to glean what's really going on in the ship.

Also, as he liked to impart, it's healthy for the crew to see their captain in all areas of the ship, even places he doesn't really need to be. It helps reinforce the bonds of service between leader and follower, and, if it's being done right, leadership is the ultimate service position. It can also be beneficial to morale for the men to see their captain in a casual manner, rather than having him yell at them to fix something.

As the captain of this ship, I'm responsible for every soul dwelling within. There's no passing the buck or shirking my duty. If I do that, someone might very well die. I've been lucky and only lost a few crewmembers during my tenure, mostly to accidents, but even that low number is much too high for my liking.

Am I making a mistake by allowing the *Frontier* refugees to dwell among us? Could we have tried to find a better solution? Or will everything really work out and I'm just being anxious?

Before I leave the bridge to make my rounds, I walk over to Swipt and lean my arm on the back of his chair. His fingers dance over the keys on his console as he runs a diagnostic on our thruster array.

"Can I help you?"

"At ease, Swipt. I was just hoping to pick your brain a little. What do you think about the human women dwelling with us on the *Queen*? And don't soften your answer out of concern for my feelings, please."

Swipt pauses mid keystroke, and his face scrunches up in thought. "Speaking for myself, I like the idea. A whole lot." He laughs. "And not just for the obvious reason."

I chuckle in response. "And what is the 'obvious reason' to which you refer?"

"Come on—one hundred and seven women? I'm not

much of a gambler, but even I like those odds. The crew have been talking and a lot of them think some of the *Frontier* women might be their fated mates."

I wince because his remark hits so close to home. I still haven't told Varia about my suspicions yet, for fear of disturbing our newfound connection.

"Do you think that's possible?" My query belies what I know in my heart. It is possible because Varia is my mate. I know that now, but I'm looking for a bit of reassurance I'm not crazy. "I mean, we're talking about two different sapient species here."

Swipt purses his lips and returns to his keystrokes. "I mentioned that a few times, but—you know that little grease monkey, Ilya? The cute one?"

"I am familiar with her, yes."

"Just between you and me, the first time I saw her I was like, whoa. Something clicked. You understand? I haven't kissed her yet, or even got to spend a lot of time with her, but I kind of think she might be my mate. I know it sounds crazy."

"No, Swipt. It's not crazy at all." I clap him on his shoulder. "As you were."

Lokyer glances over at me from his own console, his eyes somber under his horns. "Nothing's going to be the same,

Solair. Not saying it's going to be bad, but it's not going to be the same."

"Everything is in constant flux in this galaxy, Lokyer. Stagnation of thought and purpose has mired the Ataxians and the Alliance in their centuries-old war. The trick is not only to be unafraid of change but to take advantage."

Lokyer nods, but I can tell he's not convinced. He's the sort that needs charts, graphs, and peer-reviewed data before he'll accept something as truth.

I head out of the bridge, my footfalls echoing off the curving burnished walls. My ship is filled with the sounds of voices in conversation, which isn't anything new. What is new are the feminine voices joining the chorus and the peals of laughter that seem to come from everywhere.

Laughter. My crew and I enjoy a good rib, a good jest, but I don't remember us ever laughing so much. It's like with the women on board, we're seeing old things in a new light. I can only assume it's much the same experience for Varia and her people.

I find Zander in the guts of our primary gamma emitter array. He hovers ominously over two junior grade techs who are struggling to splice in a backup surge protector. It's always a good day when I don't have to fire our weapons, but I'm glad Zander's here to keep them up to spec.

He offers me a firm nod and then gestures at the

crewmen. "I'm pleased to announce that I've been able to reduce our power transfer loss during firing by nearly seven percent."

"Highly commendable." Zander is pretty grim for a Kilgari, so I'm not about to hurt his feelings by pointing out that seven percent isn't all that high. Anyway, our lives might someday depend upon that paltry seven percent, so I'd rather not court disaster. "Zander, how is everyone adjusting to the presence of the women on board?"

"We're professional Kilgari warriors." He straightens up. "We'll do our duty no matter how many distractions abound."

"So, the women are distracting you from your duty?"

"Not me—the other men. But I've also noticed that after the initial, chaotic clusterfuck of their arrival, crew work efficiency has risen by over fifteen percent. The men are happy, so they're working harder. Sir."

I think his quick justification might have something to do with the way he stares at the brilliant-but-eccentric Professor Thrase, but I don't say such a thing out loud. Poor Zander would be scandalized.

Leaving him to his duties, I next find my way to the mess hall. If the conversations throughout the ship are noticeable, in here it's downright raucous. Jax smiles and does his typical greeting of pointing both his fingers toward me while keeping his elbows near his torso. "Captain in the mess hall."

I stroll over to him, wincing at the tumult in the mess. It's definitely never been this loud before, but all I see are smiles and engaged expressions at every table.

"What's the good word, Jax?"

"Well, today I learned to make Salisbury steak, but I had to make a few adjustments to the recipe since we didn't have any Terran beef."

I arch an eyebrow at him. "Adjustments?"

Jax scratches the base of his horns and peers to the side. "Ah... good news, our rodent problem is a thing of the past."

I laugh and clap him on the shoulder. "I trust you to make anything palatable, Jax. How is everyone making the adjustment to the *Frontier* women coming on board?"

"Well, I think it's fantastic, personally. As does pretty much everyone else, even the ones who seem grumpy."

"Well, we're all adults here, Jax. Whatever happens, I'm sure we'll be able to deal with it." So, I'm not alone. It seems that some of my men already believe they have found "the one." Just as I have.

This could disrupt the peace on my ship. There are

roughly one hundred and fifty of us, and one hundred seven women. That will leave some of us out in the cold.

I need to speak with Varia again. As excited as I am to formalize our union and tell her she's my mate, I can't ignore the fact that all of this could disturb the harmony of the *Queen*.

And as captain, that troubles me deeply.

CHAPTER THIRTY-TWO

VARIA

"What's all this?"

Standing right before the doorway, I peer into Solair's quarters and my pulse quickens. Tiny holographic candles float in the air, bathing the room in a dim but warm yellow light, and there's a small round table at the center of the room. A crimson tablecloth has been draped over its surface and on top of it there's a small flower arrangement, white and pink roses peeking over the rim of a silver jar. And these are real flowers, not a holographic stand-in.

"Step into my chambers." Standing aside, Solair makes a slight bow and waves me in, an amused smile dancing on his lips.

"Said the spider to the fly," I mutter under my breath, not feeling entirely sure of what's going on. When Solair told me we needed to talk, I half-expected to be on the receiving end of more complaints regarding the *Queen* and its new occupants, not to be wooed with dinner.

"What was that?" he asks me, cocking one eyebrow up as I walk past him.

"Nothing," I reply awkwardly. "Just an old human saying."

Still smiling, Solair pulls up a chair for me. Surprised by his gentlemanly ways, I return his smile with one of my own and sit. It's hard to believe this is the same Kilgari who exploded into the cargo hold where we had been trapped. Back then, I thought of him as nothing more than a brute—a very handsome brute, all right, but a brute nonetheless.

"I hope this is to your liking." Taking his own seat, he clears his throat and looks at me. He looks slightly embarrassed, which makes for an odd sight. He's always so sure of himself, his entire demeanor that of a man who's never in doubt. "I made some enquiries as to what women would expect in a, uh…"

"In a dinner date?"

"Yes, that's it, a dinner date."

"Well, so far you're doing great." The smile still hasn't left my lips, almost as if it's permanently in place when I'm around Solair. "Although I gotta say, I wasn't expecting this."

"After what happened between us, is it that surprising?"

"Well, we spend half our time arguing, so I think that—"

"We don't argue. We debate," he corrects me, shifting his weight uncomfortably. "I mean, there's a little friction at times, but we're running large crews here. I think that's to be expected." Reaching to the side, where he has a small side table, he grabs a bottle of wine and pours some into our glasses. "A vintage red from Luvon. Hard to come by these days. I was saving it for a special day."

"A special day, huh?"

"Yes, that's what this is," he says, all of his self-assurance returning to his voice. As he speaks, he removes the silver domes from our plates to reveal an elaborate dish. There's an elongated purple fillet covered with an orange sauce with perfectly lined rows of a vegetable I've never seen before flanking it. The scent alone is enough to make my stomach rumble with hunger, and I immediately suspect Marion's involvement in this.

"And why is this a special day?" Reaching for my glass, I take a sip out of the wine, allowing its sweet oaky flavor to coat my tongue. And to think that not long ago we were diverting distilled water out of the cryopods so we wouldn't die of dehydration.

"Because I've finally come to terms with what you mean to me." He stares into my eyes. He doesn't flinch, nor does he seem uncomfortable with those words. If anything, he looks more relaxed now that he's said them, as if a weight has been lifted off his shoulders. Taking a deep breath, I lean back in my seat and look down, allowing his words to echo inside my head. I want to tell him that the same is true for me, that I've made peace with what I feel toward him, but it's not easy.

"Are you sure?" I ask him, biting on the corner of my bottom lip. "I'm bad news, Solair. If you think I'm some perfect woman who always knows what she's doing, if that's what got you interested in me..."

"You are perfect." Reaching for me, he lays his hand on top of mine, gently squeezing my fingers. "But that doesn't mean you'll always know what you're doing. I don't. Half the time I'm pretending."

"It's not just that," I continue, all my fears and doubts bubbling to the surface. "I'm afraid that when you look at me you see someone virtuous and brave, someone who always does the right thing, but... that's not me."

"What do you mean?"

"I know you think you've got a pretty good idea of who I am, but truthfully, there's so much you don't know. There are reasons why I'm so such a confrontational hardass. I grew up the oldest of a large family—seven children, to be precise—in a military family, so from a young age I've been used to taking care of others. Both of my parents were part of the IHC fleet, so usually, only one of them was home with us at any given time and it fell to me to act as the missing parent."

Solair watches me with kind, yet intense eyes, as if he's been waiting a lifetime to hear my story. I'm encouraged by his soft gaze and even though I'm never really comfortable talking about my upbringing, I press on.

"When I got older, my parents often both went out on missions and left me in charge. I learned very quickly that managing a family of seven was not easy. There was homework to help with, meals to cook, clothes to wash. At the age of fourteen, I was essentially a mother and father to my siblings, the youngest of whom was only two years old. I think I've become such a strict, regimented person because of that. You can't run a household that large without becoming a little neurotic. And then, because it was the only thing I knew and the only way out of being an adult before my time, I joined the IHC Marines at sixteen."

"So young," Solair comments, and I can tell he almost can't fathom the thought.

"I was just so tired of taking care of everyone and, being a navy brat myself, I already knew what I was getting into. I signed up the day after my sixteenth birthday and never looked back. Until the day I saw combat on Horus IV. The

Alliance and the IHC had just entered into the Titanus Vox Accords. It's a miracle I survived it when so many didn't. It messed me up for a bit and I left the navy as soon as I could—honorably discharged. I simply couldn't do it anymore," I tell him.

Unbidden tears form behind my eyes at the thought of how many friends I lost on Horus IV, but I take a deep breath and push them back down into the recesses of my heart where they belong. I've shed enough tears over that battle, and I don't want to ruin this moment between us by dissolving into a blubbering mess.

"There's nothing for you to be ashamed of, Varia. The loss of just one soul is often difficult to process. I can't fathom that many at once. If my entire crew were killed… I don't know what I'd do."

"Entire crews were killed during that battle. It was literally hell."

"Every sapient being in the known galaxy has heard about Horus IV, Varia. Everyone knows what you've gone through."

"Being arrested and waking up in the cargo hold and having all these women to take care of… it just brought back Horus IV for me all over again."

I haven't spoken about Horus IV to many others because it's nearly incomprehensible. Most can't wrap their minds around a loss that large, but Solair—even though he hasn't experienced it himself—as the captain of a large crew can. The thought makes me relax, a little more at ease with telling him more of my background. I realize with a sudden start that I want him to know me—all of me.

"I worked here and there. One by one, I lost touch with my siblings. Most of them moved out to the Outer Colonies in search of a better life. My parents passed away and I drifted. Worked whatever job I could find. I lived on Novaria for a time. Went to Earth. Didn't like the paradise that people say it is. Found a transport to Erebus and began black market dealings. Made some pretty good money."

"You're talking to smuggler. I know what it takes to survive."

"Do you know how I ended up in that cargo hold in the first place? I was arrested," I say, finally looking up to return his gaze. "I used to have some dealings in the black market. I'd fence stolen tech here and there, trying to make ends meet, or I sold and resold whatever I could put my hands on. I'm not a good person, and that's what landed me here."

"Is that supposed to be a deal breaker or something?" His eyebrows knit together. He lets out a small chuckle and then leans back, waving one hand at the four walls around us. "You are not responsible for the loss of your unit on that blasted Horus IV. You didn't kill them. The galaxy has gone mad. And in case you haven't noticed, you're aboard a smuggler's ship and I'm the captain here. I'm not exactly a holovid hero either. So, stop trying to find excuses, Varia. I know who you are and I..." He gives a slight pause, almost as if he's trying to look for the right words, and then gives my fingers a gentle squeeze. "I love who you are."

"I'm not used to that," I find myself saying, "love." Pursing my lips, I take another sip of the wine, hoping the alcohol will give me some liquid courage. "I spent all my life trying to survive, and I never really had the time for a relationship. In fact, I had already given up on it. It didn't strike me as something important, or as something I needed to have."

"Is that still true?"

"No, it isn't," I admit. "After I met you... well, things have changed. I'm not sure of anything anymore, Solair. I don't know what my place is in the universe anymore, or what I'm supposed to do with my life. The only thing I'm sure about is that I need you in it."

"This is why I've brought you here," he whispers although there's strength behind his words. Setting his silverware down, he rests both his elbows on the table and locks his eyes on mine. Something in his gaze makes my heart tighten, and my breath catches in my throat even before he continues speaking. "Have you ever heard of the mating bond?"

"The mating bond?"

"It's an old myth, dating back to the Precursors and their lessons they taught my people. We preserved them in something we call the Elder Scrolls," he explains. "A long time ago, the Kilgari didn't choose their mates. They were chosen for them."

"By whom?"

"Fate," he replies with a shrug, a small smile on his lips. "These special fated mates were known as *jalshagar.*"

"Fate chose?"

"Through lips entwined a mate is found, forever and ever the two shall be bound. That's a passage from the Elder Scroll of the Kilgar. I knew these words but never truly believed until I finally came across you, and when we kissed that first time, I..." Taking a deep breath, he gives himself a little encouraging nod. "You are my mate, Varia. I've known it since that first kiss. You are mine, just as I am yours."

I don't say anything for a couple of heartbeats, my mind working hard to digest everything he has said. Fated mates? Now that's a concept I thought to be nothing more than legend, something to tell your children while tucking them into bed. And yet, Solair's right. That first kiss revealed the naked attraction between us, sealing it in place.

Fate brought him to me. To soothe my aching soul.

"Why didn't you tell me before?"

"I wasn't sure how to tell you," he admits. "I didn't want to add to your stress."

"Everyone's stressed here," I laugh, squeezing his hand back. "There's no privacy for those who need it. Tempers are flaring. And yet, most of the women are happier than they've ever been."

"Does that include you?"

"What do you think?" Pushing my chair back, I walk around the table and stand before Solair. I place both my hands on his shoulders, and then lean down and kiss his cheek. "I've never been happier, Solair, and you're the one to blame."

"If that's the case," he says, slowing rising to his feet, "then I'll gladly take the blame."

Leaning in, he crushes his lips against mine.

CHAPTER THIRTY-THREE

SOLAIR

Our lips meet and I feel it again.

It's hard to describe. The feeling is strange and ethereal, but there's no denying it's real. It's almost like opening your eyes after you've just woken up and your brain still hasn't dragged your memories out of the shelf; it's like sunlight falling on your face and warming your skin, absolutely no baggage at all to cloud the experience. It's a feeling of belonging and connectedness, one that can't be broken.

"I feel it too," Varia whispers against my lips, and for a moment I wonder if she's reading my thoughts. Pulling back from me, she places both her hands on my face and looks into my eyes, a timid smile on her lips. "I knew there was something about that kiss, but I didn't know how to put it into words. But it's as you said—a mating bond."

"It's more than that."

"Yes," she breathes out. "It's love."

Her lips return to mine before I can say a word more. Our bodies melt into a tight embrace, our hands exploring the warmth of each other's skin, and our kiss grows frenzied with each passing second. Whatever remained of dinner turns into a forgotten detail, and we glide across the room as I lead Varia to the bed.

I pull her shirt over her head, the rising curve of her breasts immediately drawing my attention, and my heart beats almost too rapidly. Boiling blood rushes through my veins at neck-breaking speed, and a furious heat takes over the space between my legs. As my flesh turns hard, my two erections straining against my trousers, it becomes almost impossible to remain in control.

Unclasping her bra, I lean in and kiss that patch of smooth skin in the valley between her breasts. I push her down onto the mattress, my lips climbing up her right breast, and I suck her hard nipple into my mouth.

"Yes," she moans softly, one of her hands holding me by the horns as she keeps me in place. I continue kissing her breasts, enjoying the taste of her skin, but that's not enough for me. Laying one hand on top of her knee, I move my fingers inward, only stopping when the palm of my hand is pressed between her legs. She immediately thrusts against my hand, eager for more of what I have to offer. "Oh, yes."

Finally allowing some of my madness free rein, I push her pants down her legs, only stopping when she's lying on the mattress with nothing but her black panties. I hold my breath as I reach for them, carefully massaging her over the drenched fabric. When she moans again, I can't help myself. I pull her thong against her outer thigh and tear it off her body, revealing the wet and delicate skin between her legs.

I don't even hesitate.

I dive into her like a hungry predator, fitting my mouth against her aching pussy. Running my tongue up and down the length of her wetness, I suck her inner lips and caress them eagerly. It doesn't take long, though, before I focus on her clit, whipping her pleasure bud with the tip of my tongue. I do it mercilessly, each stroke of my tongue making her voice rise in pitch.

"Don't stop. Don't stop," Varia pants and cries out all of a sudden, and I oblige. Redoubling my efforts, I keep devouring her sweet wetness, only slowing down once she has arched her spine, her entire body becoming as tense as a nocked arrow. Hissing through her gritted teeth, she grabs me by the horns and keeps me in place as she comes, the sound of her ecstatic voice like a drug.

"It feels even better now that I know we're mates," she manages to say between hard breaths, her body still quivering as she sprawls her limbs on top of the mattress. Looking up at the ceiling, she draws one hard breath and only then does she look at me. "Unless this means you'll keep on getting better each time we do it."

"There's only one way to know." I laugh, climbing onto the mattress and lying beside her.

"Is that so?" She laughs alongside me, turning to the side and laying one hand on my chest. Moving faster than I could've anticipated, she rolls sideways until she's on top of me, her knees on either side of my waist. She pulls my shirt out, and then leans in until her forehead's resting against mine. "Maybe we oughta go for another round and see if there's an improvement."

"What other round?" I tease her. "It doesn't count when it's just you having all the fun."

"Weren't you having fun? It looked like you were."

"I was having the time of my life."

"That's better."

Reaching toward my waistline, she pulls my pants down, freeing my two hard cocks. She takes them both in her hands and, never looking away from me, starts moving her fingers up and down their length. Her strokes are absolutely perfect, and each time she reaches the top of my erections she caresses their tips with her thumb, driving me absolutely crazy.

"I can't wait," I say, these words escaping from between my lips before I can stop them. "I want you. Now." Placing my hands on her hips, I force her down, pressing the tip of my upper cock against her inner lips. She grits her teeth as I ease myself in, my thickness stretching her wide, and she draws one long hard breath once all my inches are buried inside of her.

"Don't hold back," she whispers, grabbing my other cock and angling it down. My hard shaft springs up the moment she lets go of it, nestling itself in the warmth of her backside, and I immediately know what she wants of me. Good—we're in sync. "Let's go all the way now."

"Your wishes are my commands," I tell her in a teasing tone, slightly moving my hips up until the tip of my second cock is pressed against her tight entrance. I take my time entering her, always scanning her face to see if she's in pain, and patiently slide all of my length inside her back entrance. Once there, with both my hard cocks inside her, it becomes almost impossible to think straight.

Still with my hands on her hips, my fingers digging into her flesh, I start to thrust. It only takes a couple of heartbeats before she starts to scream, ecstasy dripping off her voice, and a wild grin takes over my face as the sound of it fills the entire room. I still can't wrap my head around the fact that I have someone like Varia to call my own.

Every single inch of her is perfection made flesh.

"Harder," she begs of me, burying her fingernails into my pectorals as she tries to match my movements. Swaying her hips from side to side, she punishes my cocks mercilessly, the sweet tightness of her body making me delirious. "I said harder."

The lady asks, the lady gets.

Gritting my teeth, I start thrusting like a man possessed, giving her my all. She throws her head back, her hair cascading down her shoulders, and she surrenders to me fully. I fuck her in a savage manner, my body consuming hers wickedly. It's not long before I see beads of sweat pooling on her forehead, exhaustion taking over her body, and I take that as a sign that she's more than ready for the fireworks.

Reaching down, my two cocks still demolishing her, I press my thumb over her clit and stroke it. I do it harshly, massaging it almost too viciously, but she seems to love the attention. A long drawn-out moan explodes from her mouth and, right at the same time, her inner walls tighten around my hardness.

"Fuck, I think I'm gonna—"

"Don't think," she cuts me short. "Just do it."

One more thrust and I come undone.

We explode at the same time, our connection so perfect it should've been impossible. I close my eyes, electric fire lighting up my mind, and I exhale sharply as my cocks throb violently inside of her. Thrusting up, I offer her all of my seed, my warmth blending with hers, and my hips only relax when I'm completely spent.

We don't move. We remain locked in each other's embrace as the minutes pass us by, our hearts beating in the same mellow rhythm. Lazily, she rests her body on top of mine, her head on my chest. Kissing her forehead, I thread my fingers into her hair and cradle her head. I hold her tightly in a mate's embrace, knowing I'll never let go.

"No matter what happens, Varia," I whisper into her ear "I'll always be here."

"Always?"

"Always."

CHAPTER THIRTY-FOUR

VARIA

"Being a ship's captain has its perks." Smiling, Solair pushes open the glass door leading into his shower, the steam rising from it already covering the cramped bathroom hidden inside the Captain's quarters. It's not as luxurious as the bathroom in a five-star hotel, but it sure as hell beats the communal shower rooms for the crew.

"This is the only reason I'm with you," I tease him as I step under the running water, its warmth relaxing my muscles. Throwing my head back, I close my eyes and lazily run both my hands through my hair. "I was dying for a shower."

"There are shower rooms for the crew members. You know?"

"But the company here is better," I laugh, taking his hand and dragging him inside. He closes the door behind him and then stands directly beside me, his massive body offering me some support. Mother knows I need it—after the rough and tumble session we've just gone through, my knees need each and every ounce of support they can get.

"Well, I can't argue with that." Squeezing some shampoo into my hair, he threads his fingers into it and starts massaging it, his movements so damn precise that I can't stop myself from moaning. Yeah, he's that good. "The company here is infinitely better. So much that I feel tempted to lock the door and remain here forever."

"Where would you get your food then?"

"I could just eat you," he laughs, turning me around so that I'm facing him. He keeps on soaping up my body, his hands softly massaging my skin, and it only takes a couple of seconds before I close my eyes again.

"You say that again and I don't know if I'll be able to control myself."

"But I don't want you to control yourself."

"Yeah?" I purr, my eyelids fluttering as I look into his eyes. "Still not tired?"

"Never."

"Huh," I smile. "We'll have to do something about that."

Moving fast, I go down on my knees, my breath catching in my throat the moment they touch the tiles. To say that I'm amazed or fascinated by what's right in front of my face would be putting mildly.

I mean, I have experienced Solair's two hard gifts before, but I've never seen them up close. At least not this close. His existence is a miracle of genetics. Not only does he have two cocks, but they're both the biggest I have ever seen. I almost feel sorry for human males. No matter what they do, there's no way they can compete against a Kilgari.

"Seriously, you guys won the genetic lottery," I mutter under my breath as I reach for his cocks, the two of them going hard with anticipation. I wrap my fingers around them, the lengths throbbing against my palm, and my heart hammers against my chest. Every woman knows what the plan is once she's kneeling in front of a naked male, but the rules don't really apply when the man you're talking about is a tall golden alien with two hard cocks.

Not that I'm complaining.

Stroking him with both my hands, I look up at him and grin.

He returns my gaze, his lips slightly parted as he tries to control his breathing, and then places his hands on top of my head. He might be eager to take the lead, but I don't let him dictate my next movements. Instead, I dive forward and take one of his cocks into my mouth, rolling my lips down his length until I feel him pressed against the back of my throat.

Bobbing my head back and forth, I keep stroking his other cock with my hand, my fingers moving up and down his length in the same rhythm as my mouth. I keep going for a couple of heartbeats and then decide to shake things up. Allowing his hard member to pop out of my mouth, I then move toward his other one. I keep alternating, moving from one cock to the other, until he puts some pressure on my head with his hand, urging me to slow down.

"You're going to be the end of me," he breathes out and, as I look up, I see the lines on his face deepening as he tries to restrain himself. The thing is, I don't want him to do that. I want him to let go, to become his wild and ferocious self.

"Don't tell me you're already tired," I tease him, slowly rising to my feet but keeping my hands on his erect cocks. Stroking him at a mellow pace, I go on tiptoes and brush my lips against his. I pull on his bottom lip with my teeth, enjoying the soft groan escaping from his lips, and offer him the most devilish grin I have. "It's fine if you're tired. We can stop."

"I don't think so," he growls, suddenly reaching for my wrists. Grabbing them, he forces me to raise my arms and pushes me back, only stopping when I'm pinned against the wall. With both of my arms trapped over my head,

Solair holding me tightly by the wrists, I can do nothing but surrender to him.

Pressing his body against mine, his two cocks against my inner thighs, he leans down and kisses me. He does it in a gentle manner, slowly parting my lips with the tip of his tongue, and the frenetic rhythm of my heart mellows out for a second. Hidden inside the whirlwind of lust that has taken over, there's another storm, one made of passion and love. And to think I'd already given up on those things.

"You're insatiable. Aren't you?" he whispers against my lips. "You can never get enough."

"That's me."

"You've met your match, then," he continues, finally letting go of my wrists. Moving his hands down the side of my body, he takes them to my hips and pulls me up and into his arms. He does it fast and effortlessly, almost as if I weighed as much as a feather, and I react on pure instinct alone. I throw my arms over his shoulders and lace my legs around his waist, my eyes locked on his as I do it.

"Prove it," I tease him. "If I've met my match, you have to—"

He doesn't let me finish.

Before I'm through with my sentence, he places one of his cocks against my entrance and thrusts, no mercy or softness to his movement. His thick length enters me in a savage way, and Solair threads his fingers into my hair and stops me from throwing my head back.

"Keep looking at me," he orders me, and something in his voice turns me into a wet mess. Against all odds, against the laws of biology itself, I've become even wetter than I already was. It's as if my body is sweating lust and ecstasy. "Don't look away, Varia."

I don't.

I keep my eyes locked on his as he fucks me, each of his thrusts sending me higher and higher until I'm touching the ceiling of heaven itself. Even though my eyelids feel as heavy as concrete, I don't dare close them. I remain trapped in Solair's gaze until I reach the breaking point, my whole body burning from the inside out.

"Yes," he whispers, "come for me."

One final thrust and I explode.

I finally throw my head back and close my eyes, a violent scream rising up in my throat and exploding in the air. Every single muscle in my body twitches and trembles, ecstasy whipping at every fiber of my being. Right now, I don't think I'm capable of remembering my own name. My brain is busy processing the pleasure that's consuming Solair and me, and whatever exists outside of it has become a mere detail.

"Holy fuck," I mutter as he finally puts me down, my head spinning like a blender. As my knees threaten to buckle under my weight, Solair comes to the rescue and holds me up. "What in the galaxy was that? I'm shaking all over."

"That was round two," he laughs teasingly. "Didn't you say you were insatiable?"

"And I am," I reply. "But for the first time in my life, I'm satisfied."

"Just satisfied?" His lips twist. "Not that great of an endorsement."

"Oh, shut up," I laugh, playfully punching his wall of a chest. "You know what I mean."

"I do, Varia. I do." Taking one step forward, he scoops me into his arms and kisses my lips. "I know what you mean. Now let's tuck you in, shall we? You must be exhausted."

"Only if you promise me to breakfast in bed for tomorrow."

"It's promised."

Sweet mercy.

I'm the luckiest girl in the galaxy.

CHAPTER THIRTY-FIVE

VARIA

Of all the times I've been in the *Queen's* mess hall, it's never been this subdued. Part of the reason is that there's only roughly a dozen sapients sitting together at two long tables, making the chamber seem hollow and empty.

Another reason is that everyone, Kilgari and human, can sense the change in the air. The captain has gathered us here for an arcane purpose—one that's known to me, as it pertains to me.

Solair's senior staff are present in totality. Kintar and Jax I've dealt with more often than the rest, but their expressions remain inscrutable nonetheless. Swipt, the pilot with an easy smile and an easier manner doesn't seem concerned, but then again, he never does. Grantian seems very uncomfortable and keeps shooting me confused glances. The task-minded Zander sits next to the flighty pilot, finding a way to brood even as he munches on some of the crisp cookies Jax has prepared. Montier is engaged in a three-way conversation with Ilya and Nicari, which I believe is about the tricky process of cryopod awakenings.

Last but not least, Lokyer munches on cookies and stares around the room. This is the first time I've seen him off of the bridge, so maybe he's getting his sightseeing in while he can.

Solair asked me to gather up what I consider to be the "leadership" of our refugee band. In my mind that includes the aforementioned Ilya, Marion—whom I've begun to consider our quartermaster, even though she keeps trying to horn in on Jax's mess hall territory—Fiona, and Thrase.

I've also invited Lamira, partially because her presence is soothing to me. Also, I need a representative of the *Frontier* survivors present. Lamira talks to everyone with an ease I've always envied, and if anyone can feel the pulse of the mixed crew, it's her.

Lamira nudges me with her elbow and leans in close, not quite whispering but clearly uncomfortable with breaking the almost cathedral like stillness. "Do you know why Solair has gathered us here?"

"Yes, but I think I should let him explain it, out of respect."

"Oh, you're so mean." She elbows me in the ribs, but her easy grin belies the attack.

I perk up a bit when I recognize the approach of Solair's long, booted stride. He sweeps into the mess, wearing a rich blue tunic with a v-neck that displays his chiseled torso. Between his alien dress, his golden skin, and the horns on his head, he almost appears like a Greek god come down from Olympus to grace us with his brilliantly handsome face.

But then he gets that goofy grin on his lips and the image is dispelled, replaced by something more profoundly appealing. Solair is no aloof supernatural deity removed from his humanity—if that term applies to an alien. Rather, he's the quintessential man of the people, able to put others at ease with just a glance or a touch of his hand on their shoulder.

"Why does everyone look so grim? This isn't a funeral ship."

Nervous chuckling rises up from the mixed crew as Solair settles himself roughly in the center of our half circle. He puts his arms akimbo and encompasses each of us with his gaze in turn. I can't help but notice how his eyes soften when they meet mine, just for a moment.

"I'm sure you're all wondering why I've gathered you here today, and it's not to form a betting pool for this season of the BBL. Now that we've merged our two crews, we've all had to make a lot of adjustments and I'd just like to commend each and every one of you for performing at such a high level during this difficult transition." He chuckles at himself and scratches the base of his horns. "I sound just like my father." He waits for the ripple of laughter to fade before continuing. "Look, I've always played it fast and loose with the chain of command. Everyone knows that. But one thing has always been true; Grantian is my first mate."

Solair turns his gaze on the somber giant and smiles. "And that will continue to be true moving forward."

Grantian's relief is so palpable it actually makes me feel better, too.

"So Grantian is my first mate, but he, like the rest of us, has little experience in dealing with two distinct groups— women and humans. Well, guess what? Now we have to deal with one hundred and seven sapients who happen to be both. So, I'm officially appointing Varia as our Liaison Officer. She's going to help guide us all—me included— through these tricky waters."

His gaze grows narrow for a brief moment.

"But she's still part of the chain of command. If Grantian or I are not present she's in charge, and I'll tie the first tongue that wags against her in knots. And even the first mate and I are going to be very deferential to her opinions because, quite frankly, she's a damn smart woman, with military experience and lots of time spent on starships. If she weren't qualified, I wouldn't appoint her. Period. Our relationship has absolutely nothing to do with it. Anyone who doesn't like serving under her is more than able to cycle out at the next port."

Solair's gaze softens again, and he laughs softly.

"Now that I've gotten that out of the way, we can celebrate her promotion in the time-honored, traditional way. Jax?"

The cook sits there nodding and smiling for a moment, before his eyes suddenly go wide.

"Oh shit. The champagne." Jax rushes over to his pantry and disappears inside. His cursing and the clink of glass echo out into the mess hall proper until Marion chuckles and gets up from her seat to go and assist. In short order the two of them emerge from the pantry with two bottles of spirits and enough glasses for everyone.

"Congratulations, Varia." Lamira and I clink our glasses together, and the white champagne changes hue to a shade of rich lavender. "Wow, that's cool. Hey, Jax, what kind of champagne is this?"

"Well, it's not technically champagne because it doesn't come from Earth, and it's not made with grapes."

Marion frowns right before she's about to sip from her glass.

"Then what's it made of?"

Jax turns toward her with a sheepish expression on his golden face. "Ah...Alzhon swamp nuggets."

"Swamp nuggets?" Marion purses her lips. "Is that a kind of grape?"

"Uh..." Jax can't meet her gaze. "Sure, it's like...grapes."

Solair saunters over to me as I sip my drink. My eyes widen at the surprising flavor. It's sweet without being cloying, with just enough minerality to balance itself out, and it has a smooth finish. I don't know what swamp nuggets are, and maybe I don't want to, but this champagne is fantastic.

"Are you feeling under pressure yet, beloved?" His smile is only half as warm as his gaze.

"Always, but with this crew and you at my side, I think I can handle it."

Solair brushes his thumb across my cheek and kisses me softly on top of my head. "My love, you can handle anything. I wasn't kidding when I said you were the only person capable of doing this job."

I look out on the mixed crew as they converse, joke, and generally mingle. It seems to me that no matter what star you call your own, a smile is a smile, laughs are still laughs, and a gentle touch can still make everything seem all right with the galaxy.

The weight of the burden of responsibility falls across my shoulders and I have a brief anxiety attack.

"We can't screw this up, Solair. Too many people are counting on us, both human and Kilgari."

"Then we won't screw this up." He puts his arm around my shoulders and squeezes me tightly. "I'm not saying we won't make mistakes, but when we do, we'll rectify them quickly. Don't worry, Varia, we're going to take good care of them. Together."

I squeeze him back, and then I remember something I heard when I was speaking to the *Frontier* refugees the other day. "There is one thing we should probably address."

"What's that?" he turns a worried frown toward me.

"It seems that with so many people on the ship, finding areas to express our love for each other physically may be difficult."

"Ah." He grins and lifts a finger in the air. "I know exactly what you're talking about. Perhaps we can, er, arrange an area of the ship where we could pair and be discreet?"

"Maybe, or we could always tie a sock around the doorknob."

Solair tilts his head to the side, his brow furrowing in confusion.

"I'm sorry—what?"

I laugh and pat his flat belly.

"Solair, my dear, there's a lot you still have to learn about humans."

CHAPTER THIRTY-SIX

SOLAIR

A few days have passed since I announced Varia as the human liaison of the crew of the *Queen*. The ship is running more smoothly than it ever has, and I do believe it's partially thanks to her. Together, we've managed to integrate one hundred and seven human women with one hundred and fifty Kilgari nearly seamlessly. I'd be lying if I said I wasn't both proud and impressed, and not only with Varia's efforts, but everyone's.

Honestly, of the entire amalgamated crew, she and I spent the most time arguing with one another. The others, while having certain understandable disagreements, have gotten along relatively well from the outset. I don't think Varia will ever not irritate me, but she does it in a way I find most affectionate. She's always seeing things I don't, always picking up on things I've never even thought of, and sometimes it irks me that I didn't catch the issue sooner.

It appears we're unparalleled equals in strategy, physical combat, and annoying one another.

But I wouldn't have it any other way. She definitely keeps me on my toes, and the good thing for us is that after an argument we always make up in the hottest ways imaginable. I'm a lucky bastard—some days, I can barely keep up with her insatiable sexual energy.

Not that I'm complaining about that, of course.

At first, I was worried that the crew wouldn't take kindly to my promoting her to a leadership position—especially Grantian, as he takes his role as first mate very seriously— but I think they see how valuable she is. As a commander, she's fair and honorable, and never favors her girls over the Kilgari. "What's good for the goose is good for the gander," she always says, even though I have no idea what that means. I think it's something about equivalency between the sexes, but not knowing what a "goose" or a "gander" is, I can't be sure. I'll ask her one day. I know she'll find my lack of understanding of human sayings both amusing and adorable, as she always does.

On the days she doesn't join me on the bridge, she's tasked with ensuring the crew, Kilgari and humans alike, have everything they need and mediating any issues that may arise. She also keeps track of our supplies, making sure we have enough of everything for everyone. The increase in rations alone was gargantuan. I can scarcely believe human women eat so much.

We make supply runs often, as we need to stock up in a clandestine manner. With the women wanted by the IHC, the ship's roster can't reflect that they're on board. If we purchase or trade for more than necessary, merchants may grow suspicious, and the last thing we need is anyone reporting us to the authorities. The *Queen* is a good ship, but she's not outfitted for combat. If we're to be hailed by an IHC vessel, I'm not sure how we'd escape.

There's certainly no easy place to hide one hundred and seven women on board, and definitely not the ones still remaining in the cumbersome cryopods.

But that's a problem for another day.

Most days, however, she shares command with me on the bridge, confiding that she doesn't like to be away from me for hours at a time. Even though she's not a natural navigator and Lokyer already holds that position, she loves learning about the galaxy. She's never been this far out in it before and she revels in visiting new worlds.

I love observing her as she observes the dark, glittering wonder of space, and I cherish her presence at my side. The stars cast their light into her gorgeous brown eyes and set her skin aglow. She's the most beautiful creature I've ever seen and I'll never grow tired of looking upon her face. Indeed, Swipt has often ribbed me for becoming lost in a long gaze as I stare at my mate, completely oblivious of anything else happening around me.

I must say, I never thought it'd be possible for me to be so completely gone on a female, but I wouldn't change a thing.

Although I enjoy it, having a mate has been a little difficult to get used to. Not because of anything Varia's done, but because the Kilgari hadn't observed the practice for generations. It was always a real concept in our culture, but it was almost impossible to believe it still existed in any form. Whatever the reason, I'm glad the universe seems to be pushing toward its reappearance in history. There must be some importance as to why we're returning to the ways of the Precursors. I just haven't figured it out yet.

I completely understand why the Kilgari shifted focus to a matriarchal society, but I can't believe I don't have to share Varia with any other males. In fact, when I mentioned the idea to her, informing her of the polyamorous practices of my people, she seemed completely horrified, exclaiming that having one male to attend to was enough. Apparently, females in human culture often have sexual encounters with various partners, but once they pick the person they want to spend their life with, it's only one. They call it *monogamy*—something I quite like the sound of.

In fact, Varia and I have been enjoying speculating on which of our crew members will be next paired with a mate. Many have already shown promise. Fiona and Montier are currently engaged in a series of surreptitious glances between each other as she chats with Varia about the possibility of hacking into the shipping logs of the IHC to try and find out any information about why the women were taken, and I've noticed Grantian observing Lamira more closely than I've ever seen him observe any other female before. I wonder which of them will pair next.

I've decided the best course of action to keep the women's whereabouts hidden is to remain out of the League, away from the reaches of the IHC. The plan is to journey to M'Kal for another supply run, as I have trusted contacts there who I know will look the other way if I add questionable supplies to my cargo.

Swipt is just about to engage us into superluminal speed when an alarm sounds, blaring loudly enough to jolt me to attention.

"What's going on?" I waste no time leaving my seat to look over Swipt's shoulder at the flight control panel.

"Give me a minute." His fingers tap furiously at the screen

as his brow furrows, as if he can't figure out exactly why the alarm went off.

Fiona approaches us quickly with Varia close behind.

"Need a hand?" I can tell by the look on her face that her thoughts are moving a mile a minute. She's had quite a bit of experience on various vessels, so I've no doubt she'll be able to quickly identify the issue.

"Be my guest." Swipt pushes his chair back and allows the tiny female to encroach in on his space. I think he rather enjoys the view of her taking control of his domain, but he doesn't say a word about it.

Fiona's hands are a blur of motion as she pulls up screen after screen of the *Queen's* flight systems. I can tell the precise moment she locates the issue, as her eyes light up with a kind of spark I've only ever seen in Swipt's when he's excited.

"The warning occurred because Swipt attempted to push the ship into a higher velocity when there isn't enough energy reaching the core. Currently, it appears that it's all being diverted to... the med bay?"

Her statement isn't so much a statement at all, more like a confused question. She's right to be perplexed, as there's absolutely no reason for the majority of the *Queen's* energy to be filtering into the med bay. None whatsoever, unless...

Varia's voice is quiet and her eyes are wide as she asks, "Do you think there's something wrong with the cryopods?"

I pick up one of the communicators, about to patch down to the med bay when Nicari's voice comes through loud and panicked.

"We've got a situation down here with the pods. I think you'd better send someone right away!"

"You told me he knew what he was doing! Damnable oaf!" Varia exclaims, already rushing to the door of the bridge.

I know better than to respond. The scent of her increases with stress and the air is positively saturated with it, so I keep my mouth shut and follow her, hot on her heels.

I'm not sure what will greet us when we arrive, but I have a feeling it's nothing good. As we hurry down to the med bay, her hand reaches out for mine. We'll face this new situation as we have all others since the first day we met.

Together.

———

Did you enjoy *Rescued by the Alien Pirate*? Not quite ready to let go of Solair and Varia just yet? We couldnâ€™t let them go either so we wrote a fun bonus scene for you guys and you can get it FREE here: https://bookbit.ly/kilgari1bonus/

Want to know when the next book in the Mates of the Kilgari series is released? Be sure to register for Celia & Athenaâ€™s newsletter here: https:// bookbit.ly/athenacelia

---

If you enjoyed this book, please be totally awesomesauce and leave a review so others may discover it as well. Long review or short, your opinion will help other readers make future purchasing decisions. So, go forth and rate our level-o-awesome!

ABOUT THE AUTHORS

CELIA KYLE

Ex-dance teacher, former accountant and erstwhile collectible doll salesperson, New York Times and USA Today bestselling author Celia Kyle now writes paranormal romances. It goes without saying that there's always a happily-ever-after for her characters, even if there are a few road bumps along the way. Today she lives in central Florida and writes full time with the support of her loving husband and two finicky cats.

Website

Facebook

ATHENA STORM

Athena Storm is the pen name for two authors who fell in love with writing science fiction romance as they fell in love with each other.

She's the Athena. And he's the Storm. Athena hopes that one day it won't be a boyfriend/girlfriend writing duo, but a husband/wife team. But she's not pressuring at all. Not one bit.

Science fiction is the biggest love for the writing duo, and they've been doing the writing for quite some time now, building a universe that readers can get lost and explore in. Filled with big bad alien warriors, sassy human women who give as well as they get, hilarious situations, and enough steam to melt stars!

The duo have created the Athenaverse, where all books in all series are tied together. You can start anywhere but once you do, you'll want to explore them all!

When they get married, they plan to continue writing science fiction romance forever. But again, no pressure on the marrying part. Not at all. (Not like writing Happily Ever After ALL Day won't give you any ideas on its own, right?)

Sign up for Athena's newsletter!
Like my Athena Storm's Facebook Page!
Join the Athenaverse

ALSO BY ATHENA STORM

Reaper's Pet Series:

Caged Mate

Caged Prey

Standalones In Athenaverse:

Mercy's End

Bride to Beasts Series:

Zuvok

Zerberu

Vyker

Soldiers of Hope Series:

Hope In A Time Of War

Marauder Mates Series:

Sorta Seized By The Alien

Totally Taken By The Alien

Untamed

Beauty and The Alien

Conquered Mates (An Athenaverse Collaboration with Tara Starr):

Warlord's Property

Alpha's Prey

Brute's Challenge

Alien Torturer's Pet

Champions of Ataxia Series:

Gladiator to Mate You

Hating You Mating You

Scent of My Mate

Warriors of the Alliance Series:

Yaal

Duric

Made in the USA
Columbia, SC
23 January 2021